MILAN GOTCHER

When Fortune Knocks

To my best friend and loving wife for always supporting me and my little hobbies.

Contents

Chapter 1 - MR. FROST

"Nothing worthwhile comes without effort," Damian's father always said, a piece of wisdom that popped into Damian's head at the most inconvenient times—like now as he wrestled with his necktie. He watched the online tutorial again, the instructor's Persian accent smooth and calming, as if tying a Windsor knot was the simplest thing in the world. The man in the video produced a perfect knot with effortless grace, while Damian's attempts resulted in a lopsided, too-short tie that looked comically out of place on his broad frame. With a chuckle, he imagined the tie having a mind of its own, stubbornly refusing to cooperate to spite him.

"Maybe it's the quality," he said to himself, defeated but satisfied that this last knot was the best it would be. Years earlier, his button-down shirt and tie had been bought together as a set from a discount department store. The shirt was light blue, but the tie was patterned with an array of white, light blue stripes and black diamonds over a navy field. It was exceedingly thick on one end and narrow on the other, unlike the man's tie in the video, which seemed evenly tapered.

Putting on the constricting clothing reminded Damian of his high school homecoming. He wasn't a fan of these outfits, but other teachers had informed him it was necessary to dress formally during the first day of class to gain respect from his English students.

At 23, Damian looked no older than the average high school student. He couldn't grow a beard to help with this. What facial hair he could grow only made him look more like an old teenager. He'd have to do whatever he could to seem older than he was and demand some respect from the kids in his class.

He made his way into the kitchen, munching on toast and gathering the remainder of his things. His parents had graciously allowed him to stay with them for over a year as he struggled to find a steady job. He took on whatever shorter-term substitute teaching gigs he could, hoping it would lead to something permanent. He still felt guilty about living off his parents' support but was determined to become financially independent soon.

He hopped into his beat-up car, its faded navy-blue paint and scratched exterior starkly contrasting his formal attire. It was an older model vehicle and one his father had given him back during his senior year of high school. He drove it through his college years, adding up the miles each year. Even as rust began to line its fenders, it carried him from place to place without any worries. The engine sputtered to life as Damian pulled out of the driveway, his mind racing with anticipation and nerves for a new kind of first day of school for him.

Driving through the quiet streets, Damian's mind wandered to his students. He wondered what kind of learners they would be, whether they would be eager to grasp the intricacies of literature or simply slouch in their chairs, disinterested. A nagging doubt within him whispered that maybe he wasn't cut out for this job; perhaps he didn't have what it took to inspire young minds.

Damian opened the car door and stepped out, immediately overwhelmed by the humid morning air. He saw kids wearing skinny jeans, new shoes, and graphic tees talking in small groups that stretched across the parking lot. He wiped away a light sheen of sweat from his forehead and looked skyward to see wisps of pink and orange streaks dancing across the horizon. He breathed deeply, feeling the sun's rays kiss his skin as he headed towards the school.

The school was in South Hill County, Virginia, near Washington, DC. It was a far cry from a small county. Highly suburban, loaded with manufactured homes and HOAs, it seemed tight-knit for Damian, who called this area home. It was as if everyone knew everyone around, even though that was likely impossible considering the population numbers.

The classroom was small but had potential. The flat view of the parking lot and adjoining fields only served to emphasize the narrowness of the room. The two windows, placed close together, were tiny and barred, with a wrought-iron gate across them, as if they were looking into an 18th-century prison cell rather than the open air. School desks lined the walls on one side while a whiteboard stood on the other. He would have to assign seats during class because the limited space could only accommodate five rows of seats. The classroom was small but had potential.

Damian perched himself on the edge of his chair, surveying his neatly arranged desk. He slowly spun the chair to face the window, watching as students gradually filed into the school. As he watched them, he remembered his high school days. He recalled his comfort when walking to class with his friends, safe in knowing they had each other's backs no matter what the day put forth. Now, as he looked out the window, it dawned on him how hard it had been for all of them to stay connected once high school ended. No matter how hard they tried, time and distance made it impossible to keep in touch like they used to.

Students filed into the room, some in pairs and others as individuals. Many had their headphones fastened to their heads, removing them as soon as they took their seats. The hum of footsteps and conversations filled the room until the bell rang.

Damian inhaled, shut the door behind him, and said his practiced lines. He had addressed an audience of students before, but it never felt as natural to him until now. When he was a one-day substitute teacher, all he had to do was follow the instructions left for him. Most of the time, this amounted to watching a movie or completing a project with minimal effort. However, now he was sailing solo for most of the class. It was entirely up to him to keep students engaged from lesson to lesson, which seemed more intimidating than before.

With a shaky voice, Damian stumbled through his introductory spiel. His first-period class was only half-full, and most students seemed distracted or disinterested. However, a handful of friendly faces smiled at him, and he could sense their willingness to cooperate with him during his classes.

By his third attempt, he was more confident speaking to his students. Each class was different, with some quirkier than others. As his confidence grew, so did his students' attention. By lunch, he felt renewed and ready to take the next class. It wasn't until his last period of the day that he faced his first real challenge.

It was clear he would have his hands full when the students coming into class during that final period began yelling and making jokes with and about one another. They were a high-energy group and had spent time together before. Though appreciated in most circumstances, this camaraderie could become unruly if not kept in check.

As the bell rang in a familiar tone, he began his introduction as he'd done many times before. "Welcome to your 7th-period English 11 class. My name is Mr. Frost, and it will be my pleasure to introduce you all to the world of literature." He walked around the room, posturing himself in a way that he learned would comfort new students. "We will explore many different periods of literature, and along the way, you will learn how to analyze what we have read. By the end of this year, I hope you all can appreciate the deeper meanings of novels and stories. You might have noticed I don't look like a Mrs. Martinez." The class chuckled as the others had before. "And you'd be right about that. She gave birth a few weeks ago and will be on maternity leave for the first half of this school year. In the meantime, you have me to work with. I know I'm a sub, but please don't think each day will be easy. We have much to go over, and I will grade and review your work. You still need this class to graduate, so don't think you can do what you want because I'm not here all year."

While talking, Damian scanned the room to gauge how everyone was feeling. "Guys, I don't want anyone to worry. Some of you might think this class will be hard at times, and believe me, for some of you, it might be, but I will be here every day. If you think you need extra help, talk to me. I might be able to work with you after school. If you are confused or I say something that makes no sense in class, please raise your hand and let me know. I'm human, after all, and I'm bound not to make sense here and there." The class chuckled once again.

At that moment, the worried students seemed more complacent and less stressed. Any visible stress seemed to wash away, if only for a moment. Damian smiled, recognizing this, and then explained the survey he had handed them.

"Now, you all should have received a survey from the front as you came in. I want you all to begin working on it and finish it now. It is two pages long, double-sided, and…"

The door to the classroom creaked open, shaking with the force of being pushed. A tall teenage boy wearing a green and yellow Edgewater High School hat pulled down low over his eyes, a grey hoodie, and basketball shorts stood in the doorway. He glanced around the room, carefully avoiding looking at Damian as if he didn't want to make eye contact. Despite this, Damian could sense the underlying tension in the air.

"Sorry I'm late," he murmured, "I got lost looking for the class." His friends snickered knowingly at the blatant lie, but Damian's piercing look quieted them immediately.

"Just a tad late today. When you're early, they say you're on time; when you're on time, they call you late. It's something to think about." Damian smirked as he tried to de-escalate by making a bad joke. The student finally looked up from the floor, giving Damian an unenthusiastic eye roll. "Take your seat over there," Damian said, reading from Barrett Greer's late slip. "Looks like it's front row for you today." He could tell the kid wasn't too thrilled at that statement.

"I don't want to be in the front," he said hesitantly.

"Sorry, I guess, but that's your seat. Maybe we can talk about a change if your behavior is good." Mr. Frost spoke awkwardly, sensing the tension between him and the boy. He turned away from the boy and faced the class to demonstrate that he wasn't about to argue this point while also trying to remember where he had left off.

"I'm not sitting there, sir," the boy said as Damian walked away.

Damian turned around and said, "I'm not offering you a choice. Your seat is in the front."

Barrett confidently strolled to the back of the classroom and plopped himself down in a chair, arms crossed in defiance. "I'm not moving from here. What are you going to do about it?

Damian's heart raced as Barrett's sly grin taunted him, daring him to take charge of the unruly class. He wanted to establish control on his first day but didn't want to seem too harsh. The students' expectant gazes only added to his indecision, leaving Damian unsure of how to handle Barrett's blatant challenge. He knew he had to make a move, but fear and doubt held him back.

As they stood locked in a battle of wills, Damian couldn't shake the feeling that he had seen those bitter eyes before. The piercing blue gaze bore into him like hot coals, sending shivers down his spine. Every detail was etched into his memory— the sharp angle of the brows, the slight crease between them, and the intense glare that seemed to hold all the anger in the world. The familiarity and intensity of those eyes only fueled Damian's discomfort, leaving him to wonder what memories they triggered within him.

The boy's unwavering conviction mirrored his own, making him question whether he was doing the right thing. But he couldn't back down now. He needed to assert his authority, even if it meant playing his ultimate card—the phone on his desk. He was told by the other teachers earlier in August that if a student gets too out of hand, he could always call for a security officer to escort the student out of the class. They'd be taken to a solitary place to cool down. As his heart raced, he held the phone to his ear, trying to convince the boy to see reason.

"I'm not moving," the boy sneered. Damian sighed; he knew he had to act, or else his class would understand that rebellion against authority would be tolerated. He could feel them watching, judging, and waiting to see what he would do next. From the corner of his eye, he saw the boy's clenched fists, steeling himself for a fight. Damian forced himself to hold the student's gaze—he wouldn't be backing down this time.

He reached for the phone, dialed the office, requested someone escorting a student, and hung up. The phone felt heavy to Damian, like a giant boulder. Barrett sat in his seat, slumped over, his hat covering his face. The class was dead silent, and no one made sudden movements as if a dangerous animal was loose in the room.

As the security officer escorted Barrett to in-school suspension, Damian couldn't help but feel a mix of embarrassment and guilty relief. He was relieved that the troublesome student was out of the classroom, though he couldn't shake off his guilt and disappointment for resorting to such measures on the first day of class.

As he handed Barrett a survey to fill out during his suspension, Damian hoped that this small act of defiance would make him feel better about the situation. But deep down, he knew it was a Band-Aid solution to a much bigger problem that likely would reappear several times over the next few months. Despite his inner conflict, Damian proudly taught him to stand up to a defiant teenager.

After every student left his class and the final bell rang, Damian reflected on his first day of teaching. For the most part, it went very well and surprisingly quickly. He only had one student act out, and the rest behaved themselves, or at least were manageable. Still, Barrett's outburst worried him. Would he have to deal with this kid all year? The thought brought him some unwanted stress.

He began to pack up his things, and while doing so, his attention was caught by a loud knock at his open classroom door. There, he saw the very familiar face of Nash Anderson, the principal of Edgewater High and the man who hired him for this job. Mr. Anderson was also one of Damian's high school administrators when he was still in school. Back then, they were close, with Mr. Anderson being someone he could turn to for advice in his teenage years. They greeted one another, approaching to shake hands.

"Good to see you, Damian! Or should I say Mr. Frost now?" With a warm smile, the old professor extended his hand and hugged Damian. Age had etched lines into his face, but his eyes sparkled with kindness and wisdom. As they broke apart, he asked, "How was your day?" He asked in a gentle yet authoritative tone. He cared deeply about his students' well-being and success.

"Good, good. The day went by as smoothly as possible. I have a good feeling about this year, Mr. Anderson." Damian smiled, trying not to hide his anxiety.

"Well, that's good to hear," Mr. Anderson replied with a giant smile. Damian continued packing, thinking the conversation was all but over. "So, what happened to you and Barrett Greer? Not often that a student is sent out of the class on his first day.

And one of our star athletes nonetheless."

Damian took a deep breath before speaking. The last thing he wanted was for Mr. Anderson to learn about the incident in his class. "It's true; he did come late and refused to follow my instructions," Damian explained. "But I hate involving security; it makes me look like the bad guy." He paused, torn between wanting to maintain order and not wanting to cause trouble for the new student.

"I see." Mr. Anderson did not seem to like the answer. "Yes, Barrett was this way last year and the year before. It reminds me of someone." Mr. Anderson spoke as Damian gazed off into the parking lot.

Damian quickly responded, "I guess people handled him better," to divert the conversation. With that attitude, man. He did refer to me as sir, though; that was nice." Damian said, still looking out the window.

"Barrett can be a handful, I agree, but he will come around. He's a hell of a quarterback, too, and you should see him run track. He won regionals in the one-hundred-yard dash and nearly missed winning in states."

"You sound like a fanboy," Damian said jokingly to Mr. Anderson.

"Well, he does bring a lot of attention to the school. We won a school spirit award from the county last year, and they gave $10,000 to our athletic programs. I'm confident Barrett's performance on the field, court, and track was the reason. Winning transforms a school. He's a true winner." Damian nodded as Mr. Anderson continued. "Trust me, I've seen a ton of kids like him. He reminds me of a handful of friends you hung around with back in your day, so I think you can help guide him in the right direction. You understand?"

"Yes, sir. I get what you're saying. I'll do my best, but I can't make him do the work. I only have so much sway." Damian responded.

Mr. Anderson fixed his gaze on Damian, his face a mask of severity. "I know your situation," he stated firmly. "Mrs. Martinez won't return until February, so you must demonstrate your capabilities. Don't allow one unruly student to ruin this chance. Understand that this is an opportunity to showcase yourself, and if you do well, there could be a permanent position for you by June or connections to other schools for future job prospects. After all your schooling and all the other substitute jobs you've had, this is your moment to shine, but it's solely in your hands. I can't guarantee anything for you if you can't handle it. So, please, get things under control before I have to."

Damian's face appeared engaged as Mr. Anderson spoke. Inside, his mind was a jumble of thoughts, unsure how to respond. He wanted to promise his best, yet felt doubt. "I'll... I'll try my best, sir," he said, his voice hesitant.

"Fantastic! Oh, I also came here to deliver Barrett's survey to you," Mr. Anderson said as he handed it over, grinning as if there was something funny about the situation.

Damian stared in awe at the sheet of paper and waited for Mr. Anderson to leave before reviewing the survey. Barrett even attempted the study, which was a small victory for him.

But then he realized that each of Barrett's written replies repeatedly ended with the exact mocking phrase.

"Suck it, bitch."

Chapter 2 - DAMIAN

Damian's father looked at his three children seated in his vehicle. He spoke calmly but with a hint of urgency, "Time waits for no one, children. Remember that."

It was a sticky August morning, and even before the sun rose above the horizon, you could feel the humidity in the air. It was Damian's first day at Crossroads High School and Lee's last year of high school, something he wasn't as excited about. In the middle, half asleep, sat Mary, who couldn't contain her excitement over starting middle school all summer. She had already mapped her route from the street corner to her first class and knew exactly what she would wear; she talked about it endlessly.

His brother Leroy, he preferred Lee, shifted around in the front passenger seat, removing the hood of his red sweatshirt from his head as they waited at the stoplight in front of their school. He was thin and had a buzz cut that almost made him look bald when it was freshly cut.

He was a four-year starter for the school's varsity team, and he often said that cutting his hair so short made him more aerodynamic on the court. Damian was skeptical of this, but the results spoke for themselves. Several scouts were reaching out to him, and with it being his senior year, eyes were undoubtedly on him to perform. He was also quiet, often reserved from making comments unless provoked by his family and friends.

Damian's heavier frame wasn't made for basketball. He struggled through practices, pushing himself to be better but never quite reaching the level of his teammates. Football was more his sport, though he still liked to shoot hoops with his friends when he had a chance.

His father continued, "Before you know it, you'll be dropping your kids off at school, reminiscing on your high school days and feeling old like me. Learn something while you're here. Believe me, the years go by quickly." He said all this with a smile that Damian felt never left his face. Even when things were bleak, his father always found a way to smile.

"Come on, Dad, let's hurry a bit. I want to talk to some friends before the bell rings." Lee said impatiently before placing his headphones over his ears.

Still half asleep, Mary twisted and stretched out her arms, attempting to wake up. She certainly wasn't a morning person. Her pale pink dress and pigtails still made her look like a child, but hearing her speak was different. She was louder than either Lee or Damian. She cursed, which their mother hated, and wasn't afraid to give her opinion. She could stand up for herself and wasn't reliant on her older brothers like other girls.

"Wake up, girl!" Damian's father said.

"I'm up, I'm up. Stop yelling at me." Mary said, yawning.

They pulled over in front of the high school. Students started trickling in, and Damian looked for anyone he recognized. "Have a good day, y'all; hop on out now." His father said.

The car doors opened with a soft click, and the two of them

stepped out onto the sidewalk. Damian scanned the bustling crowd, searching for a friendly face amidst the sea of strangers. As his father's car drove away with a hum, he turned and took in the sounds around him. The joyful chirping of birds echoed through the air, mingling with the excited chatter of students reuniting after summer break. He breathed in deeply, feeling the anticipation building inside him for the adventures that awaited him in this new place. With a smile, he couldn't wait to see what was next.

But he couldn't help but feel like he was missing something. Then suddenly, it hit him. "My backpack!" He shouted, startling everyone around him. Without a second thought, he turned and ran after his father's car and desperately called out, "Dad! Stop!"

He pumped harder and faster as the car rolled away until it eventually stopped in response to Damian pounding on the window with all his strength. After gasping for air, he stood up and saw his dad trying his hardest not to laugh. Embarrassed, Damian opened the door and yelled, "What are you laughing at?"

His father replied, "We're not off to a great start, are we?" Now fully laughing, his sister, now wide awake, joined in on the fun.

"Nice job, Damian!" she said in an annoyingly squeaky voice.

Damian wandered the halls, doing his best to find his first-period classroom. When he finally arrived, he saw that he knew only one other person in the class. Fortunately, it was his friend and teammate, Jared Hall.

He squeaked through the door as the bell rang, arriving on time. "Shut that door, please," the teacher said, pointing at Damian. "Anyone who comes through that door is now late to class." The teacher's voice was raspy and cruel.

His teacher, Mr. Fritz, stood coldly at the front of the class, directing students where to sit.

"Great. Assigned seats." Damian thought to himself.

Though he doubted the opposite was true, Damian remembered Mr. Fritz very well. He had attended several meetings with his mother regarding Lee's "classroom behavior." Mr. Fritz was an old school, no excuse, no matter how valid, and stick-in-the-mud kind of teacher. He glared coldly at students, seemingly expecting them to be up to no good. Even as Damian approached the podium to be assigned where to sit, he felt the cold, judging stares from his new algebra teacher.

"Name," Mr. Fritz asked, not even looking at Damian.

"Damian Frost, sir."

Still not looking up, he grimaced and said, "I know that name." He grimaced again, "You have an older brother, don't you? Lee, correct? Hopefully, you'll perform better than he did."

"Yes, sir." Damian sheepishly replied.

"Good. You'll be in Row A, Seat 1."

"The front?" Damian whined.

Mr. Fritz looked up, pale blue eyes locked on Damian, and a shiver ran up the young man's spine. His eyes were so pale that they were almost white. A person could see their reflection within them like a black screen on an old television. "Yes, Mr. Frost, will that be a problem?"

"No problem at all, sir."

Glancing down at the clipboard in his hands, Mr. Fritz concluded their discussion like he had with all the other students he'd spoken to—a low-pitched grunt.

Being compared to Lee was nothing new to Damian. They

were siblings, after all. In middle school, he liked being compared to Lee; it gave him some credibility among his friends. It is as if even knowing someone in high school instantly made you the cool one. But now it was different. Lee had built up quite the reputation around school as a slacker and a kid who would likely skip more than a few classes during the year.

Damian was different. Doing well in school came easy to him. He hardly had to pay attention most of the time to earn a B and preferred attending class. Even still, the shadow of Lee would hang over him among some teachers. Mr. Fritz was a good example of this.

He took his seat and did his best to listen as Mr. Fritz gathered himself for his first day of school speech to the class. Soon, though, Damian's attention dwindled, and he began to think about what he would do after the school day. He imagined himself outside, talking with friends and preparing for football practice. Everyone was excited because they would have their first official game this week.

"Welcome class to another school year. If you've read the board, which I'm not sure why you wouldn't have by now, then you'll know my name is Mr. Fritz. This is Algebra 1, and we will learn all about…" Damian's focus drifted once again. Mr. Fritz's voice was now little more than background noise.

Damian's eyes searched the room and finally landed on a poster on the classroom wall. It was of a student looking down at a paper, contemplating a worksheet. A quote hovering over the student read: "No one who gave their best ended up regretting it." Damian liked the quote and opened his math notebook to write it inside the notebook's cover.

Mr. Fritz addressed the class as Damian's eyes again

searched the room for something to occupy his mind. Finding nothing, he focused on a specific part of the whiteboard and imagined himself on the field, dominating whoever was before him. He'd fire off as soon as the ball was snapped, bulldozing or outmaneuvering anyone out of his way. He thought about nailing some poor kid square in the chest while they weren't looking for a tackle, grabbing a fumble, and running the ball into the endzone himself.

The crowd would cheer, and he would see his teammates jumping excitedly. Then, the best-looking cheerleader would come over to him and say… "Mr. Frost!"

Damian was shaken back to reality, "Uh… Yes?"

"What was I saying just now?"

Damian felt his face flush and beads of sweat dotted his forehead as he tried to make sense of the teacher's words. He stared blankly at the whiteboard at the front of the room and felt a wave of panic wash over him. How could he have drifted off into a daydream on his first day? He cleared his throat and pushed out a shaky, "Ah… You were discussing the syllabus?"

Mr. Fritz sighed, shook his head, and said, "Wrong. Please try to pay attention, please." Damian sat there embarrassed as he heard Jared giggling across the room. Suddenly, there was a knock at the classroom door. Mr. Fritz slapped the folder he was reading from shut and went to open his classroom door. His eyes were not pleased.

As he opened the door, Damian was happy to see that another of his good friends, Theresa, had knocked. She was one of his best friends and, for some time now, a slight crush of his.

Theresa wore a short-length dress with white flowers decorated on it. She had dark auburn, almost red hair and was one of the most intelligent people Damian knew. She knew so much more about every subject than any of their friends. She was the kind of person someone could pour their heart out to about any topic, and she'd be there to listen and maybe even comfort.

"Miss, uh," Mr. Fritz looked down at his roster to see who was unaccounted for. Theresa Perez. Is that correct?" She nodded yes. "Why are you late on the first day of school? Where were you?"

"My dad's car broke down, and we had to…" Theresa said. She wasn't accustomed to being talked down to by a teacher, which showed on her face. She looked both shocked and appalled to be being scorned by Mr. Fritz.

"I've heard enough. Take your seat. There is no excuse." Mr. Fritz said dismissively.

"Yes, sir…" Theresa smiled awkwardly at Damian as she passed his desk and sat in front of Jared at the other end of the classroom.

"Now, class, take out your textbooks, and let's start by reading Chapter One."

Luckily for Damian, Mr. Fritz was the only teacher he could see himself having problems with. The rest were fine as far as teachers go. However, this didn't prevent Damian from worrying about the school year. Each teacher explained what would happen during this school year, and in every class, Damian felt overwhelmed by what they said. Each class had a massive list of topics and readings that would be accomplished by the end of the year.

Damian's gaze shifted from the clock to his notebook, where a never-ending list of assignments stared back at him. He ran his fingers through his hair, feeling the tension build in his shoulders. His eyes darted to the door as students began to pack up their bags, signaling the last bell was about to ring. As soon as it did, he leaped out of his chair and practically sprinted out of the classroom, eager to leave all thoughts of homework and deadlines behind.

Damian went to the gym lobby and the meeting grounds for all Crossroads High School students. He looked out into the crowd, searching for his friends. Seeing them, he walked in their direction and called out to them, "Hey guys!" The group of three turned, and once they realized who had called them, they smiled and waved back.

Michael Morris, a long-time friend, and Damian's teammate, was there. They grew up in the same neighborhood, and both of their parents were friends growing up as well. Michael was the tallest in the group of friends by far. Until around 7th grade, Damian had been the tallest, and he often pointed this out at the time to their chagrin. But, seemingly overnight, Michael showed up to school after summer break, 10 inches taller than before.

Standing next to Michael stood Theresa. Damian and she had the same bus route and stop. Each day, Damian would walk her home, then turn around and walk to his home. He was unsure how that tradition started but never really found a reason to question it. They would share half his headphones while she chose the music they'd listen to walking home.

They both liked spending time with one another, which caused many to think that they "liked, liked" each other. Theresa frequently shot down these thoughts by saying, "We're just friends."

The last member of the group was Jared. He was only slightly shorter than Michael but was built thick and strong. He was the kind of person who was born with a six-pack and only knew how to play football, shoot hoops, and run track.

By far, Damian felt he had to help Jared get by in school. He needed a little more push than most. Damian also knew what his home life was like. He and Jared lived down the street from one another. When Jared's parents fought or didn't come home, he would often stay the night in Damian's room. It was like clockwork during the summertime, sadly.

The thing is, Jared was a brilliant person. He had the potential to earn A's in school and did very well socially. In a science class, Damian once saw him use his Little League highlight film to explain the various forces he distributed on the field. His problem was that he was the guy who could be egged on to do something stupid, like steal something from a 7-11 or burn a notebook on a Bunsen burner for the fun of it. He would do it without question to get approval.

Damian hugged and greeted them all. "Guys, my first day was way too long. Tell me you all had a better one." Damian exclaimed.

"Nah, man. I saw my life flash before my eyes with all these different assignments! It's too much." Jared said first. He then lost interest and began watching a group of senior girls walk by.

Theresa chimed in next, "Well, I had a good day. I met all my teachers, made good first impressions, and saw Izzy in two of my classes. Plus, the three of us are in math together. Can you believe that?"

"Ok, honors girl. We know you're going to do well." Damian said jokingly. "But you're forgetting that our math teacher, Mr. Fritz, will never let us relax in that class." Theresa sighed and looked down in agreement.

"Well, I had a pretty boring day, too," Michael said. "I just want to play our first game already."

Damian suddenly remembered football once more. "Speaking of which, we better head to the locker room. You know Coach Dean will make us run hills all practice if we're late."

Michael laughed and said, "Yeah, whatever. I can do that in my sleep. You, on the other hand, big boy," Looking at Damian's protruding belly, "may die if that happens." The group, including Damian, laughed.

"Well then," Jared turned to Theresa. It looks like we are leaving you." He smirked at her, and she smiled back.

"Good, I have better things to do anyway. Talk to you later, losers." Theresa said as she began her walk with a smile on her face.

Once a safe distance away, Jared looked at Damian and said, "Does she know how to get home from here without you by her side?" He and Michael began to laugh. Damian stood there and embarrassingly shrugged.

As they entered the locker room, they saw some juniors and seniors all talking to one another. They were whispering, and it was serious by the looks on their faces. "What are you girls whispering about now?" Jared asked.

"You guys hear about what happened to Andre?" One of the players asked.

"The senior D-End? No, what happened?" Damian said curiously.

"Well, it looks like he was with his uncle or something this weekend and hurt his shoulder badly. Might be out this season now." Damian's ears perked up at the news. He tried not to smile at an injured teammate but couldn't help himself. It meant that there was a chance he might see playing time on varsity this year.

"Why are you smiling?" Luke Porter, the senior all-conference center, asked. Damian quickly whipped the smile from his face. "You're not getting his spot, asshole. Turner is! He's a senior, after all."

Turner Tatum stood next to Luke, puffing his chest high. He was a stump of a man. Short, broad, but strong as a bull. Damian knew he could do better in the open role than him.

"Shut the hell up, Luke," Michael said, coming to Damian's rescue. "We both know that Damian is the better of the two. You don't get to pick these things anyhow." Damian smiled at his friend's comment.

"Maybe not, but the coach does. I know he'll see things my way." Luke sneered.

The two stepped up to one another, getting into each other's faces. Though Michael was the taller of the two, Luke was older and more experienced. The two stared at each other intensely for a long moment, neither flinching.

"That's enough, boys." Coach Dean, the varsity football coach, said, appearing seemingly out of nowhere. "Get your gear on. You have fifteen minutes until practice. If you want to fight, we can hit the boards."

"Nah, that's ok," Michael said. "I'll start working on routes with everyone else." Even he was not dumb enough to do any hitting drills with Luke. Luke was strangely fit, athletic for his size, and surprisingly fast. Michael's skinny frame had no chance in that battle.

"That's what I thought," Luke said with a troll-like smile.

"We'll see who's left smiling by our first game." Damian thought to himself. "I'm getting that spot, and I don't care who's in my way."

Chapter 3 - MR. FROST

Damian was typing away, his fingers tapping steadily on the keyboard. He carefully checked each grade he had collected over the past three weeks against the range Mrs. Martinez had left him with and was satisfied they were in line. As he scribbled notes next to some of them, he noticed more than a couple of students he would need to check up on for the upcoming week. Damian continued to update the school's database, adding an activity to ensure the syllabus was satisfied.

"At the end of the day, people are going to make and live with their decisions, " his father would say. Now more than ever, he found his father's idioms insightful.

Damian studied the onscreen information regarding Barrett, who had returned to class and was following the rules. For a time, it seemed like things were going well. Unfortunately, Mr. Anderson was right. Barrett showed up that first week but failed to appear for the next few weeks. Damian tried not to take it too much to heart; after all, Barrett was only a kid. Still, it stung; Damian wanted all his students to be excited about being in his class.

Right after the day's final bell and before he finished entering grades into the school's system, Damian encountered Barrett conversing with his pals in the corridor. When Damian drew near, Barrett appeared startled.

"Where've you been? I haven't seen you in class this week."

"Oh, I-I've been sick." He said while his friends all snickered at the comment.

"Really? Not too sick to miss practice, I see. Mr. Anderson and I had a good conversation about that. I hear you're pretty good out there." Barrett stopped, turned around, and looked at his teacher, giving Damian the same look from their first encounter. His friends looked at each other awkwardly.

"Yeah, I guess so. Coach thinks I can play in college." There was an awkward pause. "Why?"

"No real reason," Damian answered. "But you need to come to my class. I know English isn't for everyone. I know that not everyone likes to read or dive into a story. But you need to pass the class to graduate and be able to play at the next level. Football or not, your education shouldn't come last."

Barrett nodded his head, seeming to understand what his teacher was saying. "Ok, yeah, sure. I'll be in class on Monday, I promise." He said as he made his way down the hall.

The following Monday, Damian stood before his students with no Barrett insight. Disappointed, he still had a class to teach. "So, we talked about stories last class and how we can gain insight into the culture of the societies the author lived in by analyzing them. We will take that idea and start reading our first work of literature."

A collective sigh spread around the room quickly at that remark. "Come on, guys, you're going to like this one. There are sea monsters, dragons, and Viking-like people partying," Damian said as he passed out their first text, which he printed out the same morning. "We're going to read Beowulf, a story about a man who became a legend. Now, please remember, you only get one of these. Not that I can't scan more, but I would prefer not to destroy another forest to print as many sheets of paper as needed for another stack."

Then, out of the corner of his eye, Damian saw the door swing open and turned to see Barrett walking through the door. "Nice to see you today, Barrett," Damian said, smiling and ignoring the fact that the student was late. Barrett didn't say a word but did take a packet from his teacher and sat at his correct seat.

"Now our main character is a man named, wait for it, Beowulf." Damian turned on his projector to show a slideshow he had made. "Please pull out your KWL sheets and make them as we go. First, fill in what you know about Viking culture and what you might want to learn through the story."

Damian faced his class, giving them time to think and fill out their forms. KWLs help students track their learning by having them write down (K) what they already know, (W) what they want to learn, and (L) what they learned in the lesson. While in college, Damian picked up this activity and thought it would be helpful.

Once seeing that a good number of students had finished writing, Damian began again. "Ok, so to give you some information before we read, this story begins by covering some history of a group called the Danes. They lived in what we now call Denmark, and in the story, they are attacked by a beast known as Grendel. Beowulf is not a Dane; he is from a different group of people called the Geats, whose people live in what we now call Sweden. He is summoned to help the Danes with their monster problem. Now, I'm 90% sure that none of you knew that information, so fill in that information in the 'L' section."

The classroom was silent and tense as Damian finished talking. The scratch of pens on paper was all that could be heard. Suddenly, Barrett, who rarely spoke up in class, raised his hand confidently. The rest of the students turned to look at him in shock, and Damian himself couldn't believe it. He cleared his throat and said, "Yes, Barrett?" Everyone's eyes were on Barrett as he asked his question, the air buzzing with surprise and curiosity.

"Is this going to be anything like when we read The Odyssey back in 9th grade? Like a guy and his crew sailing around and dealing with monsters?" Barrett said curiously.

"Good question," Damian said. "Yes and no, I guess, is the simple answer. Both are hero stories where the hero goes on grand adventures. They both seemingly have supernatural strength and huge flaws that cause problems for them. Both deal with monsters, that's certainly true. However, Beowulf is more independent than Odysseus. His motives, we'll come to see, are, well, selfish. He wants glory, whereas Odysseus wants to get home in one piece. So yeah, very similar. Good connection, thank you, Barrett."

"Cool. I liked The Odyssey. Odysseus was badass."

Damian laughed awkwardly, "Well, first watch your language, please, but I'm glad you liked it. I think you'll like this one as well."

Damian continued his presentation, happy with Barrett's positive response. He split the students into small groups, assigning each group an area to focus on for the coming weeks. Damian assumed that the workload wouldn't be too strenuous—no more than a chapter or two per week—but he was met with sighs and groans from his students as they shuffled around to find their assigned spots.

"Now, you're going to have readings to do at home, some-times even worksheets, and you guys will take what you learn from home and apply it in class. That means everyone needs to chip in so your group can get the most out of this. Does that make sense?" The students nodded. He continued his lesson, teaching the class more background information about Beowulf.

Damian leaned forward, mustering enthusiasm as he ex-plained Beowulf's plot to his students. He couldn't help but think that this classic epic was outdated and uninteresting, a sentiment he often felt about the entire literature curriculum. Most everything they'd read was the exact text he read in high school. As he flipped through the textbook, he couldn't help but yearn for more modern and relatable texts to engage his students. But he knew that decision was out of his hands and higher in the education system.

Damian was, however, happy to see that the school's version of the text was in modern, simplified English. Though the poetic language was lost, the story bits were all present. He only needed to express the text's main ideas and hope the students understood the significant concepts.

After the final bell rang, Damian asked Barrett to stay back a little to talk. Barrett begrudgingly agreed, and once every student had left, Barrett asked, "What is this about? I'm trying to get out of here. Football practice is in 30 minutes. I only have so much time to get my gear and get ready."

"It won't take long. I want to talk." He took a seat next to Barrett. "Thanks for coming to class today. But I've been thinking we can meet in the middle to get you in class more. I don't want to see you fall behind like I heard you did last year."

Barrett shifted in his seat uncomfortably. "What did you have in mind?"

"The way I see it, you need to get through this year to graduate, and I want to look good to get a full-time teaching job next school year. I think we can do both." Barrett nodded his head, signally that he understood. "Let's do this. If you can come to class and turn in your homework on time, I'll do what I can to get you a solid grade for at least the first two quarters of the year while I'm here. That way, if Mrs. Martinez comes after winter break and things fall apart, at least you had a good first half of the year to carry you through the next."

For Damian, it was simple math. There were four quarters in the school year, and your final quarter grades were averaged out to make your final grades. He also knew that if he could get Barrett to come to class and turn in his homework, Barrett would do just fine on quizzes and tests.

"Ok," Barrett replied. "So, I have to do the bare minimum, and you'll make sure the rest is handled?"

"Mostly," Damian said in return.

"Ok, that works for me then. But what if I fail the test or don't know what to say in class?"

"We'll cross that bridge when it comes up. I need you to give your best effort. Your coaches say the same thing to you on the field. It's the same in this classroom."

"Yeah, they always say that. You're not that bad, Mr. Frost." Barrett said, reassured.

Damian smiled back and said, "No worries, Barrett. Let me know if you need anything. Now go on, you've got practice soon." Barrett thanked him again and ran out the door and down the hall.

As soon as Barrett walked out the door, Damian's computer

chimed. It was an alert to remind him of the meeting he had to attend after school. He glanced at the clock on the wall and saw no time to reflect on their conversation. He quickly grabbed his laptop and left for his 11th-grade team meeting.

Every other week, the team convened to strategize. The content-area experts and grade-level coordinators collaborated to ensure their lessons were on track, voice any concerns about teaching plans, and arrange a uniform calendar for all team members to follow, lest one team fall too far behind or advance too quickly.

As a young boy, Damian always thought teachers were experts at creating lesson plans. He knew that they all followed the same syllabus and covered the same topics in class, but he assumed that teachers had more freedom when choosing activities. As he began his teaching career, Damian quickly realized this was not the case. Despite the occasional minor variations here and there, lesson plans for most teachers remained unchanged from year to year. Even some of the activities Damian found in his trusty white binder seemed oddly familiar.

Damian tried to hide his frustration as he walked into the meeting room. The meeting's timing couldn't have been worse. He still needed to grade a stack of papers on his desk that never seemed to get smaller and make copies of the next class's warm-up activity. The meetings were held in the lead teacher's classroom and always took longer than necessary - a fact that Damian found bothersome. Nevertheless, the 11th-grade team leader, Giselle McGrath, oversaw moderating discussions during meetings.

Her classroom's layout was different every time they had these meetings. The first time Damian stepped into her room, desks were shaped like the letter "U", with Mrs. McGrath teaching in the center. On another occasion, desks were arranged in three groups and spread throughout the room. And now, all the desks formed a diamond shape side by side.

"How do you teach with desks set up like this? It looks like a baseball diamond," Damian thought to himself.

He had not moved his student's desks since the beginning of the year and was comfortable with rows of students, one behind another. He liked walking up and down the lanes as he taught or during quizzes. In college, his teachers suggested this was a "boring setup" and encouraged desk rotations to "liven up the room," Damian never found that to be true. He stuck with what was comfortable for him. All the same, Damian took his seat on the far side of the room, what he would call first base, and waited for the other teachers to arrive.

"Hey, Damian! How are things going so far?" Mrs. McGrath asked sincerely. She was a plump woman and very smiley. Damian could not recall a time when she wasn't bubbly. She had three kids of her own, and she made it a point to say repeatedly, "Teaching is easy, but raising children, now that's a challenge." Damian certainly wouldn't disagree.

"Everything is going fine so far. I have a few difficult kids, but I'm learning to manage them."

"Well, that's good." Mrs. McGrath smiled. "Just remember not to fall behind. New teachers tend to get too comfortable early on. Then, usually around the second quarter, they panic as assignments aren't working out how you planned, or students keep missing the class." Damian uncomfortably moved in his chair, worried that this would happen to him.

"My advice is don't panic if some students fall behind. They'll either sink or swim. That's life for you."

Damian nodded politely and smiled, though he doubted the accuracy of the statement. Some students may fall behind, but teachers should still lay a hand out for them to grab, or at least that's what Damian thought.

As the other teachers filed in, Damian greeted each one warmly. The next to enter was Michael Kraft, a large man with a thick gray beard and booming voice. He smiled at Damian and said, "Hey, Damian! How do you like teaching so far? The wolves haven't growled at you too much, I hope?" His contagious laugh echoed off the hallway walls, causing Damian to chuckle and quickly close his door when it happened.

"Not yet. But any day now, I'm sure. I feel them watching me." Damian said, smiling back.

"Well, don't let them get to you. I know I must pull my whip out occasionally." He chuckled loudly. "Just kidding." He said in a way that made Damian think that maybe he wasn't.

Mr. Kraft was a large man with a big personality. He was quirky and often ended most of his sentences with a jolly chuckle, even when it wasn't appropriate. He once told Damian that he grows a big white beard each winter and dresses up as Santa Claus to make a little money. Though bold in his remarks, Damian appreciated him because he didn't beat around the bush. As usual, Mr. Kraft took his seat in the back of the room, or from Damian's perspective, second base.

Leeanne White was the next to enter. She was soft-spoken and hard of hearing. Damian was sure she never heard anything they spoke about during these meetings because she would continuously nod even when there was nothing to agree on. She meant well, but Damian was sure that retirement would come sooner rather than later for her.

Damian's least favorite team member was the last to enter

the meeting. It was as if the entire mood shifted downward whenever she entered a room. A cold, melancholy breeze that would follow her everywhere she went. Her name was Nelly Dahl.

She tolerated zero nonsense in her class and willingly allowed students to transfer out of her classes rather than work with them to stay. In meetings, she spoke with a tone that diminished others' success. Damian avoided her like the plague, but he could do nothing on days like today.

Mrs. Dahl took her seat, third base, and the meeting began. As had happened before, Mrs. McGrath started the discussion from her desk in the front of the room like the umpire. "So, how are y'all doing?" The teachers collectively shrugged and moaned indifferently. "Very good. So, I have here the result of the first batch of quizzes," She projected the results on her whiteboard. It was a giant Excel sheet with different colors representing each teacher. Damian's color was a light teal, most likely because of his last name. He scanned the projection and saw that most of his students were on track, though he did have a few with D grades, one from Barrett.

"Right now, we look good. Some students could be doing better, but not bad overall. It's still early in the year. We have to keep an eye on them." Mrs. McGrath remained smiling.

"Not bad?" Mrs. Dahl chirped. "What are you talking about? Collectively, we have over fifteen students who are nearly failing." Damian looked at the document again and saw what Mrs. Dahl was discussing. Each near-failing student was marked in a red column, but Mrs. Dahl had the fewest in this section. "We need to change that." Mrs. Dahl said definitively.

"Well, all the students I have in the red are either never in class or too lazy to do their work." Mr. Kraft said, leaning back in his chair. "Besides, it's only six out of seventy students or so. I'm not a math teacher, but that seems right in my book. Not statistically significant or whatever."

Damian nodded in the affirmative. While he wished all his students would exceed expectations, inevitably, a few would face challenges. In college, he saw some of his peers stand up and argue against this idea; they said it was up to the educator to foster their success. But Damian knew that wasn't always true: you can't help everyone.

"I think you're both right. I have Barrett Greer, and his skipping class hasn't helped his grades. But I see some potential in him. I just spoke with him, and I think we will figure it out together. We need to keep the number of kids in the red as low as…"

"Barrett?" Mrs. Dahl snapped mid-sentence. "Barrett Greer? The quarterback that every teacher has pushed along each year?" She said mockingly. "You might as well write him off like the others. He's lucky that he doesn't have me. You know, I've been doing this for a long time, and…"

Damian thought about calling her a word his mother would not have approved of but decided not to. "I get your point," Damian said, trying not to sound frustrated. "I know I'm the green one here, but I think I can get him, and anyone falling behind will do well in my class. I won't kick them out or transfer them around to someone else."

The room fell silent, and Damian immediately regretted what he had said. But the damage was done. Damian looked away from Mrs. Dahl, though he could feel her glare burning a hole straight through him.

"Yes…" Mrs. McGrath said awkwardly. "Let's move on to the next subject. We must decide on the Shakespeare play we will teach next quarter. It's a little early, but I figured we'd get it out now." She reached into a drawer in her desk and pulled out three books. "Now we have Hamlet we can do, and I know my classes last year liked it." She showed the cover of the play to the other teachers as if no one in the room knew what Hamlet was. "Or we can do Merchant of Venice."

A small voice sounded from the corner of the room. "I would like to do Hamlet if you don't mind." It was Ms. White.

Mrs. Dahl snappily said. "I say, Hamlet; my students also like this story yearly." She looked over at Mr. Kraft with an insulting glare. "I think you can handle this one too, right?" She then stuck her nose up in the air.

"Oh, I can do that." He said in return. "I'm good with any of them."

Mr. Kraft, smiling, said, "Sounds like a plan to me."

"Ok then, let's do Hamlet. I know we're going to do well."

"What did you say?" Ms. White said with a sweet grin.

Mrs. McGrath leaned forward and said, "We're doing Hamlet! I think we're going to do well with it!"

Ms. White grinned and said, "Oh, don't worry. You can tell me later, dear. Don't worry about it." Then she took her seat once more, smiling away.

Chapter 4 - DAMIAN

The season's first three games came and went faster than Damian expected. Every game, the junior varsity team started strong, holding their own. Then, suddenly, around the third quarter, things would fall apart. A punt was blocked and returned in the first game, a fumble in the next, and Michael missed an open-field tackle in the second game to stop the other team from scoring a game-winning touchdown.

Their coach addressed them after game three and said, "Gentlemen, this is a wake-up call. Having only some of you at practice isn't enough. You need to be here every day on time if you want to succeed out there! It's sort of like school; it will show if you don't show up or give your best effort."

The JV team returned with a vengeance in their fourth game—they dominated from start to finish, ending with 28-0. Damian put his all into it and earned 11 tackles, 3 for a loss, and two sacks. After the big win, their coach smiled and said, "Well done, boys! Look what happens when we put our heads down and work hard. Congrats on this victory. Let's keep the momentum going next week!" Even with the win and how well he played, Damian felt unsatisfied as he sat on the bus back to Crossroads High School. So far this season, Damian and Timmy split reps in practice. Still, Timmy played during the varsity games while Damian suited up in case they needed him. Up to this point, they had not, and dominating JV was not enough to satisfy him.

The bus ride home was long and noisy, which didn't help Damian's mood. He hated riding the bus and never understood why the entire team had to talk or yell simultaneously while on it. He preferred to sit silently, gather his thoughts, and listen to the conversations around him. Each conversation, or more accurately, gabbing, was what you could expect from a group of sixteen to eighteen-year-old boys.

"Damn! Katie was looking fine today!"

"Did you watch the game last night? Man, things got crazy!"

"No! LeBron James is not the best basketball player ever! Dude, do you even watch basketball?"

All Damian heard was chatter as the players celebrated their first win of the season. He stood alone, watching his team—Crossroads High School's perennial underdogs—surrounded by false hope and unmet promises. His nostrils flared with frustration as he looked around the locker room at all the boys, pretending that one victory could erase three losses and years of failure.

After getting off the bus and changing out of his gear, Damian called his mother for a ride home. As he sat waiting for his ride, watching as his teammates left one by one, he caught a glimpse of Coach Dean and Coach Anderson, the defensive line coach, talking to one another. "What could that be about?" Damian wondered.

He knew they likely were game planning for their next opponent, or perhaps it was just two adults talking about adult things. But, in his mind, Damian hoped they were talking about him, conceited as that may be. Maybe they saw something during today's JV game. "Anything is possible." he thought to himself.

Then, Coach Dean looked directly at Damian and began walking toward him. His face was uncertain, but his expression changed to a smirk as he approached. Damian felt his stomach flutter.

Making eye contact, Coach Dean called out to Damian. "Damian Frost, great game today, kid."

"Th-Thank you, sir," Damian said back nervously.

"I want to talk to you about something," Dean said, smiling wide.

Damian felt a rush of endorphins inside of him. "That must be good!" He thought to himself. He did his best to hide his excitement about the expected news.

Coach Dean was only a few feet away from Damian now. He had black hair with a small amount of gray on the sides, probably from coaching football. He looked like a weatherman when he smiled and talked to players after practice.

"Have you heard about what happened to Carlos during practice?" Coach Dean asked.

"Um, no, I haven't. You mean the offensive linemen, Carlos, right?" Damian lied.

He knew more than he led on. Carlos Vargas was a senior offensive tackle who left practice early this week with foot pain. It turned out that Carlos had broken three tiny bones in his foot during practice, probably from another lineman stepping on it. Damian was confused; however, he did not play on the offensive side of the ball. Why would Coach Dean bring it up to him?

"Well, I would like to talk to you about that. You know…"

Suddenly, a car honked its horn at the two of them. Recognizing the sound, Damian looked over his shoulder to see his mom in their green SUV. She was waving at Coach Dean, and he waved back with a smile. She couldn't have known that she had broken up what seemed like the most crucial conversation Damian had had in life.

"Ah, well. Let's talk about this tomorrow." Coach Dean said to his dismay. "I'll call you down to my office at some point. It can wait until then."

To Damian, it really couldn't. "Can it be for Mr. Fritz's class, 1st period? I wouldn't mind missing it." Damian said, hoping that he would say yes.

Coach Dean laughed and said, "No, Damian, you're not the first player I've had who hasn't liked that man. If I remember correctly, neither did your brother. Expect a note around the homeroom."

"Ok. I will." Damian said, trying not to look disappointed. "Have a good night, Coach," Damian said while walking away.

"You too, Damian."

Damian felt joy and confusion about what his coach might have to say, so much so that his mother noticed and, as he climbed in the car, said, "You look chipper. What did I interrupt?" Still unaware of the life-changing conversation, she broke up.

"Well, a person got hurt on varsity, and Coach wanted to talk to me about it. I don't know, though, because you came in and stopped him from finishing." Damian said.

"Well, that sounds big." She put her hand in the air for a high-five. "I think you might be starting soon. I have that mother's intuition. Make sure you don't get hurt out there like the last guy." She spouted off rapidly.

"Thanks, Mom, but it's not on the defense. The guy who got hurt plays on offense." He sighed.

"Oh, honey, you got to take advantage of the opportunities given. Playing on offense might lead to playing on defense at some point."

"We'll see," Damian replied.

"How was school?"

Damian grumbled, "Eh, not great. Not terrible, but not great. I feel like I'm learning nothing important, especially in math. Speaking of which, do I have to take a math class?"

Damian's mother looked at him with little concern and said, "Really? You know the answer to that. You only have a short time left in high school, Damian." She grinned back at him and noticed that he was disappointed. "You need to take it one step at a time."

"I know, Mom," Damian said half-heartedly. He did not get the desired answer and became mildly upset because he could do nothing about it. Math seemed like such a small thing in his life right now. Going to school was just something he had to do to play sports and see his friends. It was just another obstacle in his way, like Timmy and Luke.

Damian entered his house feeling exhausted, barely staying on his feet long enough to make it up the stairs and into his bedroom. He plopped onto his bed, switched on the television set, and began flipping through channels as his tired legs reminded him of their soreness. He tried to get some schoolwork done — a one-sided math worksheet and a survey on reading preferences — but soon lost focus.

Just as he was about to drift off to sleep, his phone jolted him awake with a vibration. It was Theresa calling. "What does she want?" he thought as he answered the call with curiosity.

"Hello?"

"Hey. Did you get anything from Mr. Fritz today? I thought he handed something out, but I can't find anything." She asked.

"Well, we got a sheet with some equations, but that is it. I'm sure it's not a big deal if you..."

"Dammit! No, I have to email him and let him know. I'm not going to look bad so soon in the year!" She interrupted. Damian chuckled at her reaction. "What's so funny?" she snapped back.

"You're getting all worked up on this. We just started, and it's going to be a long year. Just relax." Damian said while still chuckling.

"That's the wrong way to look at it, Damian." Her voice suddenly became serious. "Yeah, it's small in the grand scheme of things, but they add up over time. When he gives easy assignments, we need to take advantage of them. Who knows if he'll keep giving us stuff like this later? Haven't you figured that out yet?" Damian listened as she spoke.

She was the one person who could be there when he was struggling with a subject, and this fire in her made him do better in school. She continued. "My father once said that we are given few opportunities in life, and most of the time, we're too stupid to answer the call to action. I won't be that person, Damian. You shouldn't either. "

"Ok, ok, Theresa. As always, you're right." Damian said, trying to calm her down. "It's like football right now. A few varsity players were hurt, and..." Again, he was cut off.

"Oh, football should not be the most important thing in your life! Your education will take you places, Damian! Besides, I would hate to see you or any of the guys get hurt for nothing. It looks like there is an injury bug going around this year."

Damian laughed. "Injury bug?"

"It's a real thing! Like the flu, but for injuries."

"Is there a repellent for this bug? What does it look like?" Damian said as he started to laugh at her once again.

"Yeah, it's studied by doctors and invisible but deadly." Then, in a rather silly excuse for a monster voice, she said, "It's going to get you!" The two laughed at that.

Damian liked talking on the phone with Theresa. When three ways were huge, they and Michael would all hook up on the same line and talk for hours until one of their parents shut the operation down.

"I won't get hurt. I mean, it's me we're talking about. That is not going to happen. You can punch me if I do." Damian said.

"Oh, believe me, I will. You can count on that."

They talked like this for what seemed like hours. Back and forth, making fun of one another. Time flies when you're having fun. Eventually, though, Damian looked down at his watch and realized how late it had gotten. "Well, I got to at least try and finish this worksheet, Theresa. I'll see you in the morning."

"Ok then, best of luck with that. Goodnight, loser," Theresa said.

"Yeah, yeah. Goodnight, Theresa," Damian responded as he hung up the phone and placed it beside him.

Though the two of them had always talked openly and honestly with one another, Damian was nervous to take the next step and ask Theresa out. After all, they had been best friends for years – how could things change between them now? Added to that was his fear of her intense work ethic; would he be able to handle it if they were together long-term? He wanted to ask her out more than anything, but with these doubts looming over him, he had put off doing so for some time.

As Damian put the finishing touches on his homework, he could feel himself getting sleepier and sleepier. He was about to start organizing everything for the next day when an incoming call from Jared cut through the air. "What does he want now?" Damian thought, too exhausted to answer. "I'll deal with him tomorrow," he mumbled as his eyes finally shut, welcoming the warm embrace of sleep.

The following day began substantially better than the previous one. For starters, Mr. Fritz had a substitute who was a young, college-aged woman who sat at her desk on her phone, letting the class do as they pleased. Then, there was another sub in Damian's third period. This substitute attempted to teach a lesson on animal cells, but the class ignored him, and he quickly gave up his efforts. Before Damian knew it, homeroom had come, and still, he had not heard from Coach Dean.

Damian's homeroom teacher was a man named Mr. Hart. He had gray hair, a salt-and-pepper mustache, and thick-framed glasses. Mr. Hart was frank and didn't sugarcoat anything. When Damian earned a bad grade on his progress report, Mr. Hart looked at it, scowled, and told him that it was unacceptable before telling him what he needed to do better next time.

Mr. Hart greeted Damian as he entered the room, but he held a pink slip of paper this time. "Looks like Coach Dean wants a word with you in his office. Head on down, I'll mark you on time." Mr. Hart said as he handed the pass to the young man.

Damian looked at the pink slip of paper as if it were a winning lottery ticket. He was overjoyed but highly nervous.

He had no idea what his coach would say, only a hunch at best.

Walking down the hall toward the main gym where Coach Dean's office was located, he thought about himself playing significant minutes on Friday nights. It would be like when Lee started on the basketball team, and they'd announce his name so everyone could hear. He would be the star defensive lineman one day, and this was the first step toward this destiny. Maybe he wouldn't be a superstar this season, but he would be next year or the year after.

The words "Here Comes the Boom!" alongside an image of a cannon firing off a cannonball was engraved on the door of Coach Dean's office. The navy blue, red, and white, his school's colors, were strung around the sign. The school's mascot was the Cannons, an uncommon one for sure. Most schools had an animal of some kind or were something generic like a warrior, but not Crossroads High School. Damian loved it and took pride when they fired a cannon during home games.

As Damian went to knock on the door, it swung open, and Luke and Timmy stepped out of the office. They said nothing to Damian and did not even look at him. They acted as if they'd not even seen him, though their faces couldn't mask the frustrations within them. Damian told himself that he didn't care and continued into the room.

Damian saw Coach Dean sitting at his desk, shaking his head, and reviewing the film from the previous game.

"Ah, Damian. Take a seat, bud." Damian did as requested. "So, as I was saying before your mother picked you up, you know an offensive lineman position is open right now. If you haven't realized it yet, we're running out of linemen to throw out there. Everyone's catching the injury bug out there." Damian leaned forward and straightened his back, trying to remain still in his chair. "I was reviewing the film from the first few JV games, and it looks like you can handle yourself pretty well out there."

"Thanks," Damian said. He wanted to say, "Hell yeah!" but kept it to himself.

"But you still need to improve in some areas, particularly pass coverage. You're an island out there sometimes, and it would be better for you to assist the guys around you rather than stand there. I know you focus a lot on playing defensive line, but you'd be better off focusing on the other side of the ball right now." Damian sank in his seat. "I think you could be a great offensive guard." He went to pause the film that was playing on his monitor.

Damian could feel his stomach moving up his throat as he tried not to show his disappointment and worry. Offensive line? He had also played on the o-line during JV games, but that was only because he was bigger than most his age. He'd never really pay attention to the position otherwise. How was he supposed to play a position he did not know of with no prep?

"Starting Monday, you're going to be practicing with us. And if things go well, you'll start next Friday. Congrats! Not many play on varsity their first year of high school."

"Oh really, that's awesome!" Damian said half-heartedly, trying to be optimistic. "Do you think I'm ready at the offensive line? I could probably do both or…"

"I certainly do. I will have you talk with Coach Dyson before the game with any questions. He'll go over what you do on each play. I've also asked Luke to help you while you're out there. Don't worry. I'm not going to put you in a bad spot. But yes, I need you to play tonight. We have limited options. If you can hold down the offensive guard spot this season and work hard in the off-season, we'll see about the d-line next year."

"Yes sir," Damian said, worried and irritated that he'd have to work alongside Luke, of all people.

"One more thing before you go. You are friends with Jared, aren't you? I see you and Michael around him a lot." Coach Dean asked, changing the subject.

"Yes, why do you ask?" Damian responded.

"Well, I've seen him hanging out with the wrong sort of kids. If you know what I mean, I want to ensure he's headed down the right path. I wanted to see if you could, you know, keep him on track and around the right people."

Damian nodded, his eyes locked in with his coaches.

"Just keep an eye on him. With you, Jared, and Michael all being freshmen and playing at a higher level, you could all be big contributors for the next few years. But that means you all must stick together, push each other, and make each other better. And that can't happen if one of you falls to the wayside. Just keep him on track." Coach Dean finished.

"I'll do my best. He is a friend, and I'll do what I can."

Coach Dean patted Damian on his shoulder, trying to comfort him. "You're going to do great. Now head on back to class." He handed Damian a pass back to class, which Damian promptly took and left the room. He was confused but hopeful that everything would be ok. He'd have to wait.

As Coach Dean had predicted, Damian did fine at the offensive guard position that following week. It wasn't all that complicated once he started playing, though he wasn't perfect. To Luke's chagrin, he did earn the starting guard spot on the team by the time their next game began.

Early in the first quarter, Damian jumped offsides, drawing

a penalty, and missed several of his blocks. But at halftime, while sitting with the other offensive linemen, he took the time to look over the plays once more.

He even got some unexpected advice from Luke. "When you're out there, listening to the call, focus on the first parts. The rest is for receivers and whatnot. And if you're not sure what the play count is, just watch the ball. If you're behind, then you're behind. No biggy, but we can't take a penalty. You're not doing a bad job. Focus."

Damian was surprised to hear positive words from someone he usually did not get along with. It was a nice change of pace, and the advice helped Damian quite a bit.

With 1:48 left in the game, the Canons were down 17-14. Damian and the offense entered the field, ready to win the game on a last-minute drive. At the snap, Damian landed his block, driving his man out of the way, which led to a 12-yard run up the middle. They were at mid-field now, and the team reset as fast as possible to run the next play. This time, it was a pass. Once again, Damian made his block, and the pass landed, putting the team inside the 20-yard line with the clock at 42 seconds.

"We got this!" Damian thought to himself as his team broke the huddle. Damian lined up in his stance, ready to fire off. It was going to be another pass, hopefully for the lead, and he jittered with excitement, waiting for the snap.

Luke snapped the ball, and Damian fired off his stance, seemingly with no one coming through his gap. Then, the linebacker from the other side of the field attempted to pass him. Damian stepped forward, slamming his hands into his opponent's chest. He had stopped the blitz, and his quarterback could make the throw to a wide-open receiver in the corner of the endzone.

The school's canon rang out, and Damian knew the game was over. They had won their first game of the season, and Damian joined his team as they celebrated along with the crowd on the sideline. It was a night he'd never forget.

CHAPTER 5 - MR. FROST

Damian glanced up from his stack of student papers to the clock on the wall. It was already into October, yet it felt like he had been introducing himself to his students yesterday. September had come and gone in the blink of an eye, and he was nearly done inputting his students' grades for the quarter. The realization caused him to sigh as he leaned back against the living room couch of his parent's house, where he had set up a makeshift office.

He balanced his laptop on his lap while his mother cooked in the kitchen and his father sat in a recliner watching TV. Damian usually found the background noise from the television annoying, but today, it helped him focus on his task. He always did this even in college when studying or writing papers - turn on mellow music or an audible low-volume show. It filled in any empty silence and created a soothing atmosphere.

Damian studied each grade in his grade book, noting the familiar trend of those who attended class and paid attention well, while students who didn't do so fared poorly. He felt a twinge of pity for those working hard yet still struggling; it reminded him of his difficulties in school—no matter how hard he tried, math was always a C. He remembered teachers were once students too, with classes they had trouble succeeding in.

Damian had six students who were struggling to keep up. But Barrett was not one of them. Despite his attendance issues, he managed to do well on quizzes and group assignments. He earned a C for the quarter and kept his athletic eligibility in check, which delighted his coach and Mr. Anderson.

On the field, Barrett was excelling too. The news around the school was that he'd beat out the long-time record-holder for passing yards this season. And sure enough, Damian spotted him in a local newspaper photo spotlighting promising young athletes from the area.

Damian finally clicked the mouse and felt a wave of accomplishment over him. He slumped back in his chair, taking a deep breath before closing his laptop with a satisfying thud. Relaxing into the chair's cushion, he looked around the room: the bright morning sun peeking through the curtainless window, the blank walls hung with diplomas and awards, and his father sipping soda from a glass bottle and chuckling at something on the news. Damian let out a soft sigh, rubbing his eyes tiredly.

"Well, that wasn't so bad. Only one more quarter left!" his dad said heartily. "You'll make it through. Just think: 20 years later, you'll still deal with paperwork. You're learning how to roll with it now."

"Oh, please don't remind me," Damian groaned, taking a swig of his drink. "At least I get to close this chapter soon; Beowulf was a nightmare for everyone - students included. I might skip that part and show them the movie instead. Quiz them on it and call it done. Easier that way."

It was sad. At first, Damian's students were excited to read an epic adventure story. But soon into the first section, they began having difficulty understanding the story and characters or the key ideas surrounding them. Despite Damian's best efforts to explain the motifs and provide cultural context, the students' interest waned heavily. "At least no one failed. I got to hold on for now," Damian thought to himself.

"So, how's that Barrett kid doing? Still being a pain?" His father asked.

"He's doing fine. He's going to pass the quarter. I suppose we have an ok relationship now. I mean, he's not in class openly defying me anymore. Still skips from time to time, though."

"Well, that might be all you can ask for. One less thing to worry about."

"Yeah, you aren't kidding. But it's a long school year. Who knows what could happen to him? I'll be out of there by February."

"Have you spoken with Mr. Anderson about possibly being a full-time teacher next year? You got to be on the ball with that." Damian's father said as he changed the TV channel.

"I haven't, not yet, at least. I'm sure he knows; why else would I be substituting?" Damian said.

"Oh, I agree. I'm just saying you have to remind him. The squeaky wheel gets the grease." His father chuckled. "You know, you could always go into government contracting like Gretchen. You're smart, and I'm sure she'd give you a good reference."

Damian shrugged, seeming uninterested in the idea, and said, "Yeah, I guess. But I want to teach. I mean, I've spent all this time in college and subbing. Why turn back now?"

"I hear you; I do. But, just in case, you always have another option." Damian's father said before drinking his last sip of soda.

Gretchen and Lee had been married for about a year, having met through mutual friends. She worked as a government contractor, spending her days in an office with stacks of paperwork spread across her desk. Damian couldn't imagine himself in such a role; he felt teaching was much more fulfilling because it allowed him to make a real, positive impact on someone's life, no matter how small.

The leaves shimmered in orange, red, and brown collages, and Fall had officially begun. Damian was driving to school that morning when he noticed the tree had started changing colors. The air was remarkably crisp, as always during good Fall mornings. This gave him an upbeat mood for the day as he maneuvered through each class without a hitch.

The day went by smoothly, as Damian had hoped. It was the end of the unit, and most teachers, including Damian, were showing the last portions of Beowulf's movie versions. It wasn't his favorite movie, but that mattered little.

He walked into his final class period, and strangely, he saw that each of his students was wearing the same color clothing. Everyone was clad in Kelly green t-shirts, and some even had their faces painted.

"What could be so special about today?" Damian wondered. He'd been so caught working on grading papers and lesson plans that he couldn't remember if his other classes looked this way. "It is Friday, but that can't be it."

He searched the room, puzzled, hoping to see something revealing what was happening. Then it hit him. He looked up at his class and asked them rhetorically, "The pep rally is today, isn't it?" The students nodded their heads eagerly. "I forgot..." The class began to chuckle at their teacher's embarrassment.

"Well, let's make the most of our time." He looked down

at his schedule to verify the times, and as he did, he felt a pit in his stomach. He searched his desk for what he needed for today's class. He looked through his desk drawers, on top of his table, and in his filing cabinets, but it was not there. The sudden realization that he was not ready for class sunk in. He had forgotten to print out extra copies of his activities with the rest of his periods that day.

It was a simple follow-along with a worksheet for the movie, which he had meant to make more during his lunch break, but that had yet to happen. "Mr. Frost, what are we doing today?" a student called out after some time passed.

Damian spun on his heel and quickly walked toward the classroom door. He looked sideways at the figure that had caught his attention and was relieved to see it was a substitute teacher like himself – he could tell by the sticker with the name on it. "Could you please take my class for a few minutes? I need to make some copies," Damian asked. The substitute nodded in agreement, and without waiting for an answer, Damian raced down the hallway toward the copier room. His heart raced as he watched the clock ticking away precious seconds, and when he finally reached the copy room, four agonizingly long minutes had passed.

He threw the activity sheet onto the copier, inputted how many copies he needed, pushed start, and waited for the machine to do its job. He only required twenty copies of a one-sheet document. How long could that take?

He watched as the copies began to pile up in the tray. He was making good time and only needed five more copies before he knew it. But the worst happened just as he began to feel a little hope that his students would have enough time. Two words in big red letters appeared on the copier screen. "Paper Jam."

"God... Dammit..." Damian sighed to himself.

At that moment, he remembered what Mr. Anderson had told him long ago when he was about to graduate from high school. "Just calm down and breathe when things get tough and deadlines are coming up. There's nothing you can do about time. Just focus on your current objectives and keep on rowing forward."

Breathing in deeply, Damian went through the machine as the copier instructed, carefully taking out every jammed piece of paper and checking to see if the problem was fixed. When the machine started back up again, it went slower than usual. These machines seemed to break down right when teachers needed them the most.

"God help me." He thought to himself in a panic.

Finally, the machine spat out the final copied sheet, and as soon as it did, Damian grabbed the stack of paper and ran down the hall, doing his best not to make a scene. The last thing he wanted was for someone to complain to Mr. Anderson about him disrupting other teachers.

When he returned to his assigned classroom, most of his students were either talking to each other loudly or on their phones. "All right, all right, everyone listen up! Put your phones away. C'mon, y'all know better." He made his way to the front of the class. "I have our activity for today, finally. Put your stuff away; we don't have any time to waste."

He said this with a smile, thinking he had made it just in time to get something done. Then, to his dismay, the announcement bell rang, and the woman in the office said in her nasal voice, "Will all classes taking place in the English, Math, and Science classrooms please make your way to the main gym for the pep rally today? Thank you." No sooner had the announcement been made than Damian's class grabbed their things, entered, and went down the hallways.

Damian watched as they left feeling defeated. As the last student exited the classroom, he exclaimed, "Dammit, Damian!" thinking he was alone.

"Don't be too hard on yourself, Damian." a voice said from the corner of the room. It was the substitute from earlier that Damian had asked to watch his class. He was an older man and sat in his chair with a smile. "It happens. You'll figure it out."

For some reason, his words made Damian feel better about the situation, and he replied, "Thank you," while shaking the man's hand before leaving for the rally.

The gymnasium was packed full of students, entirely separated into their grade levels. The gym housed the basketball/v olleyball courts and had four equally sized bleachers, two on either side. The students on the four bleachers wore different colors to represent their grade levels. The Freshmen were dressed in white, sophomores in yellow, Juniors in green, and the senior class in black.

The energy was high, as was the noise level in the gym. Damian was a little embarrassed that he didn't remember wearing his class's color for the rally, but he was relieved that most teachers didn't bother either.

Damian remembered a time when pep rallies excited him. He remembered the excitement of being around his friends and watching the cheer squad perform, the different games being played, and the football coach's speech that rallied the school behind the team. But for whatever reason, a pep rally wasn't as fun when you were the teacher. Now, he could only think of how much time was being taken away from his teaching time.

He felt a slapping on his right shoulder as he scanned his gymnasium for his students. He turned to find Mr. Anderson next to him, smiling. "Just like the old days, huh?"

"Something like that," Damian replied smiling.

"Yeah, kids love this stuff. No matter how long I've taught, nothing excites them more than a pep rally. Well, maybe a snow day." Mr. Anderson said, half yelling to project his voice over the students. They both laughed at the honesty in that statement. "Hey, can I talk to you outside? Won't be long."

Damian nodded, trying to figure out what Mr. Anderson wanted to discuss. He followed his old teacher outside of the gymnasium. As the door closed behind them, Damian became suddenly aware of how loud it was in the gym. The lobby outside was silent except for the noise coming from the gym. "Now, I just want you to know that you're not in trouble and that I see progress coming from your room."

Damian nodded, trying to figure out where this conversation was headed.

"But I heard about the incident with Mrs. Dahl. It sounds like you commented that she wasn't too happy about. I got a chance to see the grades from your classes for the first quarter. Honestly, I'm a little concerned. Your kids are passing, but you have far too many getting by with low Cs and Ds." Damian felt a cold sweat race down the back of his neck and looked away from Mr. Anderson uncomfortably. "It was only the first quarter; it should be the easiest. Grades like that, early in the school year are scary to me, let alone the Mrs. Martinez who will have to take over when your time is up."

"What can I do to improve Mr. Anderson? I'm trying my best here, and many kids are getting it. But, yeah, I have a handful that either aren't understanding or are somewhat out of the loop. I mean, those struggling tend not to be in class or are not paying attention." Damian said, defending himself.

"I understand what you mean, but we can't have that again. You have to find a way to improve these grades next quarter before Mrs. Martinez starts in February. I know you're a substitute, but I want you to do well so that I or some other school can see your capabilities. So, I'm going to pair you up with Mrs. Dahl. We do this with new teachers typically before the year starts to give them someone to lean on when they have questions. She's got a lot of experience and I think…"

"Oh God," Damian said unintentionally out loud.

"What?"

"I can't stand to be in the same room as that woman Mr. Anderson. She's always giving her opinion and judging me."

"Well, I'm not giving you a choice Damian. Now listen to me, she has a lot of experience. It's a little rough around the edges, I get it, but she can help you with lesson planning and coming up with activities that work. You don't have to take everything from her as gospel, but you should at least listen to her. So, starting Monday, please meet with her every Monday afternoon and show her your weekly lesson plans. That way she can advise you on teaching activities or maybe even tweak a few things here and there."

"Yes sir," Damian said defeated.

"I'm going to check in on the two of you occasionally. You got this." With that, Mr. Anderson patted Damian on the shoulder once again and went back into the gym. As he opened the door, the noise spilled out, filling the lobby, and just as quickly, silence came again as the door shut.

At that night's homecoming game, Damian kept his distance,

standing alone along the field's borders and watching the students and parents cheer in the crowd. Although he would have preferred to be at home relaxing, Damian had promised some of his players that he'd be there, and he was determined to keep his word. Things were looking good for the Edgewater High School Eagles as Barrett was crushing it on offense; as is usually the case, schools schedule their homecomings when playing against a team they should beat. That way, everyone can go into the dance with a spark of morale from winning.

Of course, this isn't always possible, but tonight it seemed that this would be the case. The Eagles went into halftime up 28-0. Barrett had thrown for two touchdowns and ran one in himself from 30 yards outside the end zone.

Damian positioned himself so that the team would pass by him as they came to and from the locker room and still be able to see the field. When this happened at the end of the first half, Damian made sure his students who were on the team saw him, especially Barrett. He learned in college what he already knew from real-life experiences. It was important for students to see that their teachers were interested in their lives outside of school. Sports are the most accessible avenue for this.

As Damian stood at the fence line, watching the marching band enter the field and judging whether to head home, he heard a familiar voice call out "Damian?" to him.

He turned to see a face he hadn't seen in many years. The man was standing in line at the snack bar, dressed in faded blue jeans and a black T-shirt with the Edgewater County Police Recruit patch hot-pressed on the chest. He had a friendly disposition. Neither said a word but walked toward each other smiling. The two shook hands and hugged like family. It was his childhood friend Michael.

"Hey, I didn't expect to see you today. What are you doing here?" They separated, still smiling. "Yeah, I'm here to watch; well, I guess you could call him my cousin. I heard he was pretty good too. The little man is killing it tonight! Reminds me of us back in the day, haha." Michael, still smiling, turned and looked at the field.

"Wait what is your "cousin's" name?" Damian thought for a moment as Michael geared up his response. Michael had a large family outside of the area but couldn't think of any he'd met growing up. "I'm teaching here for now. Kind of; I mean, I'm subbing. Maybe he's in one of my classes," Damian asked.

"His name is Barrett. Tell me he's one of your students, that would be hilarious!"

Damian, dumbfounded, swallowed slowly, and said, "Barrett... Barrett Greer? The quarterback?"

"Yup! That boy's special," he said, smiling and flexing one arm. "An athlete like me. It must run in the family."

"Something like that," Damian mumbled. He couldn't believe Barrett was related to one of his childhood friends. Michael, though maybe not perfect, was a good person growing up. He went to class, sometimes caused problems, but skated through high school quickly. He even managed to land a baseball scholarship after transferring to a private school. He had a mean swing and was played center field mainly due to his athleticism.

"Yeah, he's one of mine all right," Damian said awkwardly.

"That's awesome! How's he doing school-wise? Hopefully, well, he's got some colleges scouting him out now. I think I saw a few guys wearing hats for Tech."

"Honestly, he's doing better, but still needs some work. Could we talk about it sometime?"

Michael's smile faded from his face. "Let's grab a drink after the game. We need to catch up with each other. How's that sound?" Damian nodded in agreement; it was a Friday night, after all. The two then reclaimed Damian's spot on the fence line and tried to catch up on everything happening in their lives.

It had been almost six years since the two saw each other last, though you couldn't tell from their conversations. Life has a funny way of bringing people back into our lives when we least expect it.

The last time the two spoke to each other, they were just entering their last year of high school, and Michael was leaving the area to live with his father for a time before going to college. After that summer, the two slowly began hanging out with each other less and less, losing contact outside of social media.

So much has changed since those days. After injuring his shoulder during his second season, Michael saw Lee graduating from the police academy on his social media account and thought he could do the same.

"I still can't believe you and Lee are cops," Damian said while eating his walking taco, which consisted of a bag of taco meat, sour cream, lettuce, and potato chips.

"Well, you know." Michael chuckled. "I was hopping from job to job at the time and helping my Pops out, and I saw that Lee became a cop and thought if he could, then I could. It's a respectable living, but not very safe, but the benefits are great."

"Yeah, well, teaching has not been going as expected for me, honestly. I'm not even full-time, just a substitute, but it's weird. I expected how I'd run a class and how my kids would react to the lessons, but that's not happening now. I don't know, it's tough." The second half of the game began. "Not what I expected."

"Well, I think you'll figure it out. You always did." Michael turned his head towards the field. "Come on, Eagles! Let's go!" They talked on and off for the remainder of the game.

At the game's end, the two approached the players as they went to the locker room. Many of them said "Hi" to their teacher, which made Damian feel better about everything being the same. When Michael saw Barrett, he called out to him to get his attention.

Barrett stretched his arms wide, happy about the win, and hugged Michael. But his elated face fell flat when he saw Damian in the background. He made half-hearted arm movements, like he was starting a handshake, then stopped and waved weakly.

"Nice game Barrett! You were something out there!" Michael said with a smile on his face. Barrett stared at the two of them.

"Thanks… Why are you with Mr. Frost?" Barrett said confusingly.

"Who? Oh, yeah!" Michael turned to Damian, "I can't believe they're calling you that now." He turned back to Barrett, "Yes, Barrett, this man was my best friend growing up. I don't know where I'd be without him. We ran into each other tonight at halftime, and he told me that you were one of his students. Isn't that awesome?"

"Yeah…" Barrett said. He stood there, shifting his pads around uncomfortably.

"Yeah, quite a coincidence," Damian said, breaking the silence. "Why don't you head off into the locker room." He smiled at Barrett, who, in return, smirked back. "Have a great weekend."

"Yeah, ok. Thanks for coming tonight, both of you."

"Yeah, of course! Again, great game out there. Tell your mom I came to watch. She's been bugging me to come for a while."

"Ok, I will, Mike. Thanks for coming." Barrett then ran off to join his teammates.

The two friends drove separately to a small Brazilian restaurant about a mile from the school. It was a small place on the corner of a newly built shopping center; from the looks of things, it was a popular place on a Friday night.

"Man, I don't know how you do it. How do you teach and put up with all these kids." Michael shook his head and sipped his beer. "And I'm sure their parents have to give you so much grief, too."

"I have no idea either man. I mean, some days it's great. Lessons go over well. I don't get grief from anyone. Then boom, things happen, and I'm left to figure out how to get a kid interested in whatever we're talking about or turn in their work on time. It's not how I imagined it." Damian said before gulping beer from his glass. Michael nodded, seeming to agree. "Can we talk about Barrett? I'm not getting through to him. I thought I was for a little bit, but I don't know anymore."

Michael leaned in, seeming interested in what Damian was about to say. "Is everything ok with him? Is he being a prick?"

"Well," Damian said, trying to find the right words. "Kind of, yeah. When he is in class, he can be a prick. But what's hurting him is not showing up for long strands of time and missing assignments. It's keeping his grade in a D/C- range. Granted, he can turn things around, but I don't want it to snowball."

"Dammit," Michael said. He seemed to be thinking about what to say next as he leaned back on his barstool, looking up at the ceiling tiles above them.

Damian took another gulp to top off his first glass. "And I've tried talking to him about working harder and staying after with me, and to his credit, he's been better than he was during the first few weeks of the year. But it ebbs and flows. You know what I'm saying?"

Michael leaned back forward, sighed, looked at Damian and said, "Let me tell you a bit about Barrett. I call him my cousin, but we're not blood. My aunt, Michelle, adopted Barrett a few years ago. From what I've been told, he's been through a lot. His biological father was never around, and from the sounds of it his mother lost custody around the time he was five." Damian sat there in shock, leaning forward as if to hear more. "It was drug-related, but my aunt wasn't too specific, but he bounced from foster to foster until my aunt adopted him at thirteen. He can be standoffish at first, he is to most new adults he meets, but he's opened up to us at least." Michael took another sip of his drink.

Damian reflected on the information he had gained. It made a lot more sense now. Why was this kid so rough around the edges, and why was Mr. Anderson so adamant about not worrying about him? It wasn't just his athletic ability; he must know about his past as well. However, he would be unable to say anything to Damian because Damian was a substitute teacher.

"Well, look, he's the star athlete in the school. You know how that affects kids and inflates their ego. I want to make sure he stays on the straight and narrow. "

Michael looked forward, away from Damian and down at his glass, before responding, "He reminds me of Jared... I'm not going to let that happen to him."

"I know you won't. Neither will I. So, what are we going to do?" Damian replied.

"No idea, man. I'll tell you when I figure that part out." Michael raised his hand and called the bartender over for another beer. "I wonder how he's doing. Jared, I mean. Do you have any idea?"

Damian shook his head. He hadn't seen Jared since going off to college, too. Before leaving, they'd spent most days together, but they hardly spoke once he was out the door.

They both took a large gulp of beer. "Last I heard, he had gotten locked up for stealing some electronics from Best Buy," Damian said.

"Yeah, that happened, but that was maybe four years ago. I ran into him maybe a year and a half ago now at the mall. I'm pretty sure he lives down in Richmond." Michael said, sighing.

Damian spoke, "We helped him so much during and after high school, and then one day he loses another job because of a piss test, and poof, he's gone. Off the map." Damian took another sip and realized that his tongue was beginning to feel numb.

"What else could we have done, Damian? We both were there to push him through everything. But nothing ever stuck. How long were we supposed to hold his hand?"

"I hear you, but Barrett," Damian said in a lower tone. "Barrett won't be like that. I see a kid who doesn't know how to play the game of life yet. All he cares about is sports, which I think we both understand, but he also needs to do well in the classroom. It might even take him further than either of us got."

Damian suddenly felt light-headed and relaxed, a desired effect of alcohol, and at that moment, he welcomed the feeling.

The stress from school was beginning to affect him more than he liked to admit.

The two continued talking animatedly, remembering long-forgotten moments and commiserating over recent disappointments. As they spoke, the restaurant emptied around them, eventually leaving only the two of them and the handful of servers cleaning up the restaurant. Damian eventually glanced down at his phone, surprisedly noting how late it had become. "I think it's time we head out," he said regretfully.

"Yeah, no kidding. I got to come by and see your parents sometime soon. It's been too long. Could you talk to them and tell me when would be good." He laughed.

Smiling, Damian said, "Definitely, I'm sure my mom will like seeing you."

The two said their goodbyes and went their separate ways. Damian stayed in his car and watched as Michael's car drove out of the parking lot. He sat in his car until he sobered up, before starting his vehicle and heading home.

CHAPTER 6 - DAMIAN

The bleachers were packed with roaring fans, rattling with anticipation for the year's final match. The Cannons were playing Jasper Sterling High School, and both were neck-and-neck. Tonight, only one team would prove their dominance by lifting "The Bell" – a heavy iron ship bell from the USS Sterling that was presented to the winner of this annual game. This prized trophy represented more than bragging rights for the next school year – whoever won The Bell could proclaim themselves superior to their rivals until the teams faced off again the following year.

The weather was perfect as Damian marched with his team towards the field. It wasn't like he had planned, but he was a starter now, like his brother before him. He lined up beside his teammates, ready to run onto the field. The marching band formed a tunnel for the players to run through.

The drummers began to beat their drums. It would only be a matter of time now before the team rushed the field. Then the trumpets began. Damian could feel his teammates leaning forward, bending their legs, and waiting for the rest of the band to join in. Then, there was a sudden rush of sound, and like a herd of buffalo, Damian and his teammates ran onto the field with the crowd roaring. "This is it!" Damian thought to himself, loving the moment.

Damian felt a sudden chill rush through his body. He opened his eyes to find Mr. Fritz standing over him, an icy stare in his eyes. He immediately sprang to attention, aware that the entire class was now watching him. He could feel the heat rise in his cheeks as Mr. Fritz's voice boomed in his ears: "Why are you sleeping in my class, Mr. Frost?" Damian wanted to vanish into thin air; he hated when teachers addressed him by his last name like that.

"Sorry, I'm just tired." He finally said.

"Tired? Why would you be tired? Football, I bet! You need to focus more on schoolwork Damian, not some sport." Damian sighed, having heard this spiel before. "Football will only take you so far. You need this class to graduate high school soon. Sit up." Damian inhaled deeply, aware of the stares and whispers coming from his classmates.

"Why is he like this?" Damian thought to himself as he sat in class. "Does he really think I'll pay more attention if he treats me like an idiot?"

He slumped in his chair, wishing he could disappear from everyone's sight. Then, from behind him, Damian heard a voice say to Mr. Fritz, "Leave him alone, man. He just fell asleep."

Damian swiveled around to see who had spoken up, and it was none other than Jared. It was strange enough to see him in class, as he usually only came in for quizzes and exams. But the real shocker was that he'd said something out loud during class, as he was not known for speaking much.

Jared continued, "You know we have lives outside this room. We have a game this week, The Bell Game if you weren't aware. We got bigger things on our minds than learning how to find the answer to x."

"Is it that time again?" Mr. Fritz questioned out loud. "Well, in any case, your concerns should be on things that matter. Your education is more important than a game you will only remember in a year or two. When it's all said and done, you'll…" Jared then immediately cut him off.

"Bro, shut up. Are you stupid?" The class was in shock as he said this right to the teacher's face. "Of course, it's just a game, but this is just a freshman math class. At least I'll remember the game. Man, most of us only have a stupid game to look forward to. Your job is getting us through this year. That's it. No one here is going to be a mathematician. All I need is to know how to count paper, that's all. This class is irrelevant otherwise."

The class was shocked by Mr. Fritz's abrupt change in demeanor. His face turned a deep red, and his eyes blazed with an unknown anger. He turned to the chalkboard, silently erasing the equations he had written on it. Without warning, Mr. Fritz grabbed his briefcase from the front of the classroom and stormed out without a word, leaving behind an eerie silence. Damian's heart sank as he stared at the closed door, realizing that this must be somehow his fault for falling asleep during the lecture.

The students glanced at each other uncertainly, unsure of what to do now that their teacher was absent. Some left the classroom to explore the school, while others huddled together in hushed conversations. Damian remained rooted to his chair, wracking his brain for ideas to make things right.

He scooped around the room, sure that Jared and Theresa were still in class, but he was wrong. "They must have slipped when the rest did." Damian thought to himself. "I wonder where they went."

The day only declined as it went on. During homeroom, Damian was called to Coach Dean's office and heard him say, "Damian, I told you if you worked hard enough, there would be a chance at playing the D-line this year, but I don't think that's going to happen now."

He had been pestering the other coaches about getting some defensive line reps after performing well at guard in the last six weeks. It was clear some were growing irritated with his persistence.

"Stop bugging the other coaches. There's one game left in the season. I don't want to mess up any chemistry on either side of the line right now." Coach Dean concluded, removing any hope for the year's defensive playing time.

After the meeting, Damian decided to work out his frustrations. He texted Michael and asked him to join him in the weight room at school before practice. By the time Michael arrived, Damian was finishing his fifth set of squats. The tension he had been carrying with him lifted away with each move he made. This was his sanctuary, where he could focus on lifting weights and leaving all his worries behind for a while.

"Spot me." Damian asked, "I've had a shit day." The two of them worked out together while Damian explained everything. He explained what happened with Coach Dean and Mr. Fritz and expressed his discouragement about the situation.

"I'm sorry, dude, that sucks," Michael said, trying to sound supportive. "Did he give you a reason or anything?"

"More or less… yeah," Damian said half-heartedly.

"What then?"

"He doesn't want to mess up any line chemistry, or whatever. He said it was late in the season and that I needed to focus on one position to help the team." Damian said. He knew his coach was correct in his heart, but he couldn't scratch the itch he had to get out there and prove that he wasn't just a freshman.

"Man, you deserve to be out there. But hey, look, you're a freshman on the varsity team. No one can take that from you, and you best believe that means something. You can play on defense next year, keep working hard."

"I know, it sucks you know?" Damian said with a smile beginning to emerge. It was nice to know that he had someone on his side. Ever since Michael's mom passed away many years ago, the two had grown close, so much so that Damian's mom often referred to them as "The Twins", though they looked nothing alike.

"You're like a brother to me, man," Michael said, with Damian nodding in agreement. The two left the gym and headed to practice, where they'd mostly spectate as the defensive starters worked.

Later that Friday, as Damian and Theresa walked into Mr. Fritz's classroom, the two friends saw yet another substitute teacher at the front of the room.

"Ugh… another sub?" Theresa expressed unenthusiastically. "Where is Mr. Fritz? I'm tired of doing worksheets." She had become bored with the busy work that the school provided, and at the kinds of substitutes who showed up each class. They were often college kids or elderly men and women who taught "back in my day."

Theresa wanted to be challenged, something the rest of her class did not care for. They had enjoyed taking advantage of the situation given to them by doing honest, straightforward work to better their grades in the class.

"Hello, class." The substitute said tentatively. The class looked up from their conversations to see a short, Middle Eastern-looking man who, from the sound of things, didn't speak English all that well. "My name is Mr. Elamir, and I will be your substitute today." The class, losing interest, began their conversations again, paying no mind. "Um, ex-excuse me class. I am talking… Hello?" The conversations continued.

The substitute cleared his throat and waved the crisp stack of worksheets to get the class's attention, only for it to fall flat on its face. With a defeated look, he dutifully handed out the worksheets to each student, emphasizing that they were due after class. He shuffled over to the front desk, plopped into the chair with a sigh, and opened the book he had brought as if it were his lifeline.

"I can't take this anymore!" Theresa said in a way that only those directly around her could hear.

Damian was grinning, mocking his friend's despair. "Why not? It's not like the world will end. Plus, my math grade has never been so high before! I need these worksheets."

"But we're learning nothing! How can we succeed in college if I'm not doing the math class everyone else is?"

"The way things are going, I will have my first A ever! How can that be bad?" Damian said, laughing.

"What are you talking about?" She answered. "Damian, you've gotten A's in English for like three years now." He had forgotten this fact. "You got first place in the 8th-grade poetry contest and had the best short story in 7th grade. You don't need an easy assignment. You need to put as much effort into math as English."

Damian thought about this for a moment. For a long time, he wasn't very good at any subject. It was hard for him to focus sometimes. The words on the page seemed to jump around. So, one day, he decided to write down his thoughts, and he found that writing generally came quickly.

When he was in 6th grade, his teacher, Mrs. Weber, showed him some reading techniques that helped the words not to jump around as much. Once that was fixed, he learned that he liked to read and sought books to read at home, away from his friends.

"Yeah, I guess so. But I don't like English all that much." Damian lied. "It comes easy to me."

"Well, maybe you haven't had that moment yet," Theresa said. "I mean, I didn't like Science all that much, but then I began to learn about Biology, and boom! It's my favorite subject now."

"Maybe... We'll see." Damian said half-heartedly.

Just then, a knock at the door came, and the two friends turned to see Jared stagger into the classroom. Immediately, Damian felt a pit in his stomach. His clothes were disheveled, to say the least. It was the same clothes he had worn the day before. He also looked weak, and his eyes squinted as if the light was hurting them. What was more worrying for Damian, was the smell coming from Jared. He reeked of booze.

"If you don't have a pass, I'm marking you late. You have a pass?" the substitute said, not even getting up.

"Uh, yeah... Here you go." Jared said before sitting next to Theresa.

The substitute eyed the note up and down wearily, and surprisingly accepted it, and went back to reading his book. Damian could not believe that nothing happened. Could the substitute not smell what he could from across the room? Maybe he just didn't care.

Jared had done some stupid things before, but this was the

dumbest. He was hungover and in school during Hell Week. Why wouldn't he have just skipped the day?

"What are you doing, dude? Aren't you worried you'll get in trouble? Like serious, kicked out of school type of trouble? I can smell the beer on you." Damian exclaimed quietly, not to get any more attention from the sub.

"Hey, calm down. Look, it was thirsty Thursday. My head is pounding through right now, but the beer I drank last night should be out of my system." He chuckled. "Plus, I wrote a note on my pass for the sub to read…"

"What did it say?" Damian asked.

"I wrote that I'm wearing my father's clothes, and he was an alcoholic, and that my mom would bring new clothes for me to change into later today."

Damian was amazed that his note worked, and he couldn't hide that from his face while Theresa shook her head. This insane plan of Jared's worked perfectly, even if it was a total lie. Jared hadn't even seen his father in almost a year, but somehow, he made it work.

"Come on, don't look at me like that, either of you." Theresa avoided eye contact with Jared. She must have been appalled by the whole situation. "I probably shouldn't have come in, I get it. But I just wanted to have some fun last night. Plus, I wasn't completely lying. My mom is bringing clothes. I told her I stayed at a friend's house last night." Jared said.

"Ok, man." Damian struggled to find the right words. "Make sure you stay away from the other teachers, though, before your mom brings your stuff."

"Thanks," Jared said, rubbing his fingers against his temples.

Damian sat there thinking about what to do. He decided to talk with Jared privately because this whole situation worried him, and he got his chance to do so later that day after school.

Jared sat alone on the main lobby stairs, looking at his phone, smiling, and rubbing his head. Damian walked up to him and said, "Hey man. Can we chat real quick?"

"Yeah, sure." Jared quickly exited the app he was using and switched over to his photo album. "Look at these pictures of last night. I'm telling you, I was the main attraction. Everyone wanted to talk to me! My first high school party, and man, did I spark. They couldn't even tell I was a freshman." Jared said this while showing Damian every picture he had taken.

Jared laughed and smiled in the photos, his arm thrown around a group of unfamiliar teens. He had a mischievous glint in his eye as if he was sharing a private joke with them, one that they were all in on. His classmates had grown used to this behavior; he was always the life of the party.

"Dude, isn't that a bit much? I mean, today in class, you could have been caught! Probably should go easier on all that, right?" Damian said, trying to convince his friend that he was in the wrong.

"Today," Jared scoffed. "I'll be more careful next time. But it worked out all the same." Jared said, trying to brush off the comment. "I got carried away last night. But everyone there was drinking, and I had to keep up."

"I don't get why, though. I mean, it's not like you knew them. Who cares what they thought of you..."

"I do," Jared said. "I care, Damian. You're my friend, but don't try to stop me from having fun. I wouldn't do that to you."

"I'm trying to help." Damian tried to recover.

"I don't need it. What I need is for you to butt out. Be happy that I'm happy."

Jared looked at Damian with eyes full of anger and sadness. Then without notice, Jared got up, bumped Damian out of his way, and walked toward the locker room. Damian didn't know what to do. He was trying to help his friend.

The two didn't speak while preparing for the Bell Game. Damian did his best to focus on the task and everything else to the side. The school was depending on the team to bring home a win.

As he strapped his shoulder pads on, he struggled to reach the last clip lodged under his back pad. He reached for it and twisted about, trying to pry out the clip without success. Looking over at Jared, he said, "Hey, could you help me out here? I can't reach my last clip."

Jared did not respond or motion that he had even heard the request. He continued tying his shoes and adjusting his knee pads.

"Fine," Damian said, annoyed that his friend would help.

Just then, Damian felt a hand reach up into his back pad, grab the clip, and place it into his hand. Surprised, Damian turned to find Luke standing behind him. "Thank you," Damian said, surprised that Luke, of all people, would help him.

"No problem," Luke said, "Look, I know we got off to a bad start this season with Timmy and all. But I'm glad to have you on the o-line. You've done well out there for a freshman. I hope we can be cool."

Damian didn't know what to say. Luke had not spoken much to him in the season. He thought that was because he was a freshman. Seeing Luke now, apologizing and being appreciative, was strange. Still, it made Damian happy, as if he had proven to some of his teammates that he belonged.

"Yeah, we're good. Let's get this win tonight." Damian said

as the two pounded each other's fists before the two separated to finish their game preparation.

"Well, well, we're making friends. Didn't he diss you a few months ago?" Jared said, now paying attention to Damian. This time, Damian acted like he didn't hear his friend. "Whatever, you aren't all that, bro," Jared said as he put his helmet on and began to walk to the field for warm-ups.

Damian blocked the comment out of his mind. He had more important things to worry about at that moment. They had to win the game, and Jared's attitude could wait.

The game underwhelmed Damian as it wined down to its final moments. Edgewater dominated the game. The Eagles scored on their very first play. It was a run right behind Damian's gap, straight up the middle 72 yards for a touchdown. The crowd erupted, and Damian felt the rush of pure joy as soon as the referee signaled the touchdown. But, during the next drive, they again drove down the field and scored a touchdown. Then again, each score loses its luster on the next drive and the one after that.

By the end of the game, Damian's team had won 42-0. The second half went by quickly as the mercy rule came into play, which meant that the clock kept running.

As the clock ticked down to zero, the Edgewater High School home crowd cheered while Damian and his team got in line to shake hands with the other team.

Damian looked around him, happy that they had gotten the win. His first ever Bell Game was an overwhelming success that could never be taken away from him. As he celebrated with his teammates, he couldn't help but want this moment to last forever. Mr. Fritz was wrong; this team, this sport, was more important to him than anything.

CHAPTER 7 - MR. FROST

Damian sighed as he shuffled through the papers on his desk, the cold air from outside seeping in through his cracked window. He loaded the finished exams onto his computer and skimmed each grade individually. His brows furrowed as he read out loud, "82.4%, 68.3%, 75.5%, 63%, 59%, 73.5%, 82.1%…". The results weren't what he had expected.

His students' grades were now below the expectations that his team and Mr. Anderson had set earlier in the year. To remain in good academic standing, a quarter average of 80% was needed. Damian's classes were currently averaging 78%.

At their last meeting, they determined having a big test right before winter break would be beneficial, so the long hiatus from school didn't impact scores. "We can make it our last grade before the break. A nice exam on everything we've learned in the past few months," Mrs. Dahl said. Damian understood, but that meant he had little time to review with students beforehand, making him uneasy.

Time was not on his side as Damian looked at his calendar to find that the upcoming week was the final one before the break. He had very little time left to help improve these scores and get the kids ready for a benchmark at the same time. Then, when they returned from winter break, Damian would have less than a month left before Mrs. Martinez returned. If he would impress Mr. Anderson enough to get a job next school year, now was the time.

He thought about giving out homework as well but dismissed the idea. He did not like giving out homework, grading it was more trouble than it was worth. Students didn't like it, and Damian found it tedious. At the beginning of the year, he only gave out homework sparingly. But since he started working with Mrs. Dahl, he found himself giving it out more and more. "Homework is annoying, but these kids need practice at the end of the day whether they like it or not." She would say. "Stop trying to be their friend."

Though awkward at first, meetings between them turned out to be very helpful for Damian. She showed him how she organized her lessons and kept them organized throughout the year. She also explained her style of classroom management, which was stern but ultimately fair. It had helped quite a bit, and he found it easier to keep track of projects and assignments week by week.

Initially, Damian had written Mrs. Dahl off as stuck-up and assumed she knew everything. But he soon realized she was also kind and talked about her children and grandchildren with a certain fondness. She expected particular behavior from him and his students, but their grades were still slipping, and Damian felt there wasn't enough time to make real changes.

Mr. Frost pressed his forehead against the cool window and surveyed the parking lot below. The afternoon light illuminated a group of students dressed in oversized jackets, standing in a huddle near a small clump of trees. Some of them were upperclassmen and he could tell they were sharing cigarettes, passing them from person to person with little regard for authority. Across from them, a smaller group of girls watched with giggles and whispers. Mr. Frost shook his head; the naiveté was almost too much for him to bear.

Scoping around, Damian spotted a group of teenagers atop the hill leading to the football field. They were dressed in the latest fashion trends—skinny jeans and plaid shirts—and some were attempting to do skateboard tricks on their colorful boards, which only resulted in embarrassment. At the theater exits, another group was making quite a scene with their acting out of whatever play they were performing. Exaggerated movements, facial expressions, and laughter filled the air as Damian watched from afar in amusement.

As Damian stood there trying to think of something to do, the door to his room creaked open suddenly. He turned to see Mr. Anderson rushing into the room with a clipboard. He did not seem pleased.

"Damian, we need to talk." Damian sat at his desk nervously and invited him in to sit. He chose to stand.

"Now, I know things are improving with Barrett, but I must ask you what you plan to do about your class average. I have a list of every teacher not meeting my goal of 80%, and you are on it, Damian."

Damian felt the clammy beads of sweat gathering on his forehead as he watched Mr. Anderson. His teacher from high school had always been kind and cheerful, but now he stood with an fierce focus and intensity in his gaze that Damian hadn't seen before. As he spoke, Mr. Anderson's voice was edged with sharpness, words delivered rapid-fire and without hesitation.

"Well, I'm looking at trying to incorporate a short, in-class group project or assignment to add some needed points for some students. I hope to get every student to earn a B- or better on the last quiz. If that happens, I think that I…"

Mr. Anderson, not happy with that plan, spoke up. "Listen, right now, you need to get your class average up. It would help if you aimed higher than a B-. If you aim high and the kids miss, then at least you'll be where you need to be class average-wise. But if you aim low, your kids will aim low, too. You should focus on preparing them for the benchmark, maybe have a big review day."

"I'm doing the best I can, Mr. Anderson. I'm trying to improve all my class' grades. Some are not getting it, and maybe, I don't know, something more creative might help them." Mr. Frost said defensively.

"You don't have time, Damian. You're focusing on the wrong kids. The ones at the bottom and top at this point have made their beds. The rest of them, the ones in the middle, need your attention right now. Get the middle's averages up, and the class will look much better on paper. A good example is Barrett. Why is Barrett still hovering at a C- average? You should be working with him more to improve that."

Damian stood there for a moment, not knowing what to say. Eventually, he swallowed his pride, nodded in agreement, and said, "Ok. I'll get it done, sir. I'll find a way."

Damian had never experienced much difficulty in school, usually finding it easy to earn a B+ with only half-hearted effort.

"Keep leaning on Dahl; do as she does. She's got a lot to offer. You need to handle this. C'mon, I believe in you and want you to look good when you're applying to full-time positions next year." Mr. Anderson said as he stood up and walked out of the classroom. "I'll catch you later, kid."

When Mr. Anderson left the room, Damian stood up and looked back outside the window, banging his head against the glass defeatedly. He saw the same theater group still messing around. They had fun acting out scenes in their own unique way. Damian stood there, remembering the carelessness of high school. There were no worries, no pressure, only good times with your friends, even if it was as silly as acting out some play.

As Damian looked over his schedule, an idea suddenly occurred to him. They still had Act 5 of Hamlet to read, and rather than have them read it at home and then review it in class, a much better plan came to mind. "We can act out the scenes!" he thought excitedly.

He would assign each scene to different groups, create a rubric, and give each group a class period to present their scene to the rest of the students. It was the perfect way to finish before break.

Damian sat back at his desk and began typing feverishly on his school laptop, creating a rubric that would justify a big credit plunge at the end of the quarter. This was going to be the solution he was looking for, and hopefully, one Mr. Anderson would approve of.

"My students can all do well in this. They got this! It's in their hands now." Damian thought to himself.

The following day, Damian presented his ambitious idea to the students. He enthusiastically addressed them, saying, "As you know, we're studying a play. I thought it would be enjoyable if we put on the pieces instead of merely reading them out loud. To end this unit, I want you all to form teams and act out various scenes from the play instead of reciting them."

A groan echoed across each classroom as Damian paused to gauge each class's interest. Some students lean forward, intrigued, others payed partial attention, and Barrett was somewhat present but distracted by whatever is happening out the window. "Come on guys, lighten up. It's the week before break. Why not have some fun?"

Another groan sounded, this one louder than the first. "Oh, would you rather do an essay then? C'mon, this will be fun. Now, I want you to get into your groups and review your scenes, they've been assigned on the board. You have all day to prepare, then next class everyone will present. Don't waste any time." Every other class that day had no further questions about the project. Barrett's class, of course, was different.

"What if we're not here to present? My family's thinking about leaving for my grandparents early this year." A student called out.

"Ah, good question!" Damian said as he turned to face the student. "If you are not here, a few things will happen. First, you'll fail the project, hurting your grade." More sighs came from the class. "Second, you'll likely hurt every one of your classmates in the process—all of them. We're not reading this act in class, but that does not mean there won't be a test on it. Your presentations may be the only way some of you know what happens at the end of the play." Hearing this, the students quickly organized themselves into their groups and began reviewing their sections.

Damian glanced around the room, taking in the buzz of energy as the students moved about with purpose. His gaze settled on Barrett, who was deep in conversation with his group—most likely hashing out details for their performance of Hamlet's iconic last scene. Barrett gestured grandly, and Damian could see the sparkle in his eyes—the same fire Damian had witnessed when they first read the play together. He felt a surge of optimism; his group would do well.

So far in his experience as a teacher, Damian has seen that students' actions seem to direct the class. For example, the more Barrett resisted assignments or skipped class, the more often other students did as well. The opposite was also true, which only made Damian feel better about the class project as Barrett began to practice his lines. He could feel the other students watching Barrett and taking cues from him.

Each play was to be 5-10 minutes long. This meant that all groups had to condense each scene to its essentials. Damian gave each group leeway over the language they used during their plays. He didn't expect them to use lines directly from the play but instead wanted them to break down the ideas of the lines into smaller pieces.

In all honesty, the class needed to do well on this assignment. Damian needed to show Mr. Anderson that he could handle things his way and was ready to change things up when necessary.

Damian walked around the classroom, observing each group and their progress. They only had so much time to complete this task. He approached Barrett's group to see the teen taking charge for the first time. "So, who's going to be Hamlet?" Damian asked, knowing the answer.

Barrett looked up and said, "I am." His group did not seem as enthusiastic about their scene as he did. Their scene wasn't the happiest. After all, Hamlet is a tragedy; it is the final scene in which Hamlet, along with others, dies.

"Good. It looks like most of you will bite the dust," Damian said, laughing.

"Yeah, and we fight with swords! It's going to be fun." Barrett said, grinning.

"I'm eager to see what you all have in store then," Damian said. He turned to face the class and said, "You all have the rest of the class to prepare. Good luck."

The class spent the last hour and a half working together in their groups. Damian had a good feeling that things were going to work out. The assignment was not all that difficult, but it asked the students to think about their assigned roles and be creative. The students just needed to take advantage of the opportunity given to them.

As the class began to work, Damian noticed someone standing at the classroom door. He went to see who it was and found Mr. Anderson watching the class. "Can I help you with anything, Mr. Anderson?" He asked.

"I came to see how your review was going, but I see you added another project instead. I thought we talked about this?" Mr. Anderson said, frustrated.

"Yes, but this will work too, I promise. All my classes should do very well in this project. Plus, it should help them all with the test too. I learned in college that when students interacted with their subject, they did better understand it," Damian said nervously.

Mr. Anderson stood there and looked at him. His face had no real expression, a stare that seemed worried. "I hope your way succeeds, Damian. We shall see, I suppose." Mr. Anderson said in reply.

Mr. Anderson's walky-talky crackled to life. An urgent voice spoke of a student who had gone rogue, causing massive disruptions in another teacher's class. Mr. Anderson tensed, and his eyes darted towards Damian as he said, "Have to go. I don't want to pressure you, Damian, but please stay on them so this works," before hurrying away with the urgency of his mission. Damian stood alone in the room, feeling the weight of responsibility settle on him.

During the next class period, Damian sat at the back of the classroom and watched his students play while taking notes and passing judgment on them. He found that the presentations were all well done. Some groups were better than others, but no group did worse than a B+.

"Ok, very nice guys," Damian said as he gave a thumbs-up and a smile to show every group that he approved of their presentation. You all can take a seat. Ok, looks like…" he looked down at his list of groups. Barrett's group is up presenting the final act of Hamlet. Are you guys ready?"

"Yes, sir," Barrett said as he and his group members stood up and walked to the front of the classroom. They wore no costumes, as most groups did, but they had made cardboard swords for the final sword fight. They also brought with them a sizable golden wine glass that had been painted gold for their scene. The class laughed when they pulled out their props as they had a silly appearance to them, with the swords being way too big and the cup being obscenely big as well.

Damian liked it all the same because it showed that they were willing to put in the effort to make something for their presentation. Hopefully, their acting was as fun.

As Barrett's group set themselves up, Mr. Anderson popped into the classroom. Damian saw him immediately and said, "Good timing, Mr. Anderson! You're in time to see our last scene." He grinned at his boss as if to embarrass him into staying and watching.

"Well, you did send me an email about today earlier. So, I thought I'd try and stop by. Where can I sit?" Mr. Anderson answered back.

"My desk is fine if you want, or you can sit with me and the other plebeians." Damian opened his arms to gesture that he meant the students, and to his surprise, his students even got the joke and laughed. Mr. Anderson also liked the joke and nodded to Mr. Frost to show approval.

He sat right next to his former student, and Damian began to feel the weight of pressure set upon him. "Can I see the rubric?" Mr. Anderson asked. Damian was not a fan of rubrics by any means. He didn't like the box it placed students in, but like most teachers, he bent at the knee when asked to provide one by the higher-ups.

"Sure thing. Do you want to grade this group?" Damian asked as he handed over the rubric.

Mr. Anderson took a few moments to consider the suggestion before he accepted. "Sure, why not? I haven't done this in a while, but it should return to me." He collected the rubric and clipboard from Damian and seemed relieved to be done with the job. Now he could relax and watch.

"Are you guys ready to go?" the group nodded. " If so, then please begin."

Barrett stepped forward and began by clearing his throat to say, "Our scene is the final one, and believe me, it will be tragic." Then he listed each role his group members would play. When he finished, another boy narrated in the background, guiding each actor's movement in the reenactment.

It started with the sword fight between Laertes and Hamlet. As Laertes lay dying, and the queen fell to her death via poison, Barrett began to point his sword at the boy playing Claudius.

Damian got a kick out of how dramatically the students acted. It took away from the seriousness of the scene a bit, but he didn't mind it at all. However, he couldn't tell if it bothered Mr. Anderson.

Damian looked over to see if Mr. Anderson liked what he saw. He wore an intensely serious face, taking in everything the group did. He smiled when the class laughed at Claudius' death noises or Barrett accidentally dropping his sword and having to pick it up. He sat there, watching.

As Hamlet died, Claudius stood up from his chair, explained how another ruler would soon take their place, and finished the presentation by saying, "Ok, we're done."

The class erupted into applause and laughter. They loved the performance, and by far it was the best of the bunch, mainly because of all the dying. Damian was also happy that the group did so well. Mr. Anderson was finally smiling and clapping along with the group. Damian hoped that this meant that he must have loved it.

"Okay, ok, everyone. Settle down." Damian said, standing up and holding a stack of papers. Everyone, take your seats, and let's finish the class off with the quiz I mentioned earlier. With all these great presentations, you all will do well." Each student took their seats, and Damian passed out each quiz one by one with a smile on his face. Once each student had their quiz, Damian said, "Please begin."

As the students began their quizzes, Mr. Anderson stood up and began to make his way to the door to leave. "Could we talk quickly?" he asked Damian. Damian agreed and met him outside the class full of students.

"I wanted to let you know I enjoyed watching the kids today. They looked like they had a good time. That's always good to see," Mr. Anderson said, finally smiling.

Damian looked at Mr. Anderson and smiled, liking the comment. "We'll see. I'm glad you enjoyed it."

Mr. Anderson patted Damian on the back and left the classroom. The young man contemplated whether all his hard work had been worth it as he tallied up the test results. When he calculated the class average, he welcomed the 82% with a sigh of relief. Now, he could finally relax and enjoy the upcoming winter holiday.

CHAPTER 8 - DAMIAN

The buzzer pierced the air, signaling the end of yet another JV basketball game. Damian sat on the far end of the bench, right where he had been each game night of the year—clapping and cheering as his teammates came in and out of the court. While he was talented enough to make it onto the team, he never entirely made it into a game. But that didn't stop him from enjoying what he did have—the best seat in the house.

Basketball was his brother's and friends' forte; they were lankier, taller, and more agile than Damian. They would move effortlessly up and down the court and generally dominate in their games. On the other hand, Damian was a football player - what his coach called a bruiser. Whenever he was in the game, he'd dive for balls, set hard picks, or foul hard to make the opposing team think twice before driving in the lane.

Damian and his team stood and lined up to shake hands with their opponents. "Good game, good game," Damian repeated. His team, having suffered their fourth loss in a row, slowly walked to the locker room, heads low, preparing to hear another long, drawn-out speech from Coach Jones.

Damian sat near his locker and watched as his coach strolled into the locker room last, waiting for everyone's attention.

"Guys, I think we are getting better. I can see it in the energy we have out there! We still need to fix the little things, though. We've lost our last three games because of the little things,"

Some of Damian's teammates began to nod in agreement, their faces solemn. Damian forced himself to do the same, not wanting to seem apathetic. His teammates—especially Jared—were more invested in this loss than he was.

"Jared, you played well tonight," Coach Jones continued, "But I need you to distribute the ball better. We had far too many turnovers tonight." When the coach turned away, Jared rolled his eyes.

"Michael, your defense is getting better as well. Keep it up. All of you are playing the best you can, I can tell. But we need to learn from this game. We have practice Monday in the small gym. I will be there ready to win. Let's do it, guys. Hands in."

Damian and his teammates each put one hand on top of each other. "Team on three. 1, 2, 3!" Then in unison, they yelled, "Team!"

After Coach Jones exited the locker room, Michael jokingly said, "Man, it must suck riding the bench so hard, Damian. You must have splinters on your butt?" A good number of Damian's teammates laughed at that one. Damian didn't appreciate the remark personally, but he knew that his friend was joking around.

He wanted to say something clever and funny but wasn't as witty as his friend. Instead, Damian grimaced and said to his friend mockingly, "Whatever, superstar. Keep improving that defense, and maybe we'll lose by less next time."

Damian faced his locker, ready to go home, and began to change out of his jersey when he heard his coach call out, "Damian, can you meet me in my office when you're done changing?" Damian nodded, confused about why he was being asked to meet his coach.

"Why would the coach want to talk to me?" Damian thought to himself. He assumed it was about not cheering or clapping enough on the bench; his coach was enthusiastic about that. Either way, after putting his clothes on, he entered his coach's office as requested.

To his surprise, Jared was also in the room with them. Damian didn't notice him walking in before him and was now even more curious about why they were meeting. "What's going on?" Damian finally said cautiously.

"Take a seat. Don't worry. Neither of you are in trouble." Coach Jones said. Damian took a seat next to Jared. "Now, I have a proposal for you, Damian. Jared is falling behind in several of his classes. As I told him, I planned on benching him until his grades improved." Jared moved in his seat, obviously uncomfortable and embarrassed, making no eye contact with his coach or Damian. "I want to know if you could help him. Not do his homework or anything like that but be there to do homework with him. You have a similar schedule, so you'll have the same homework, right?"

Damian furrowed his brow, trying to make sense of the words coming out of his coach's mouth. He glanced around the room, looking at photos and different awards hung on the walls, and felt frustrated. He had earned some of the highest grades on the team, but that was saying little; most of them wouldn't have passed even the most straightforward math test.

His coach continued. "I'm asking you because you two are friends, and it so happens that the study hall is starting back up after school again. Before practice, it should be going on, so don't worry about being late. Even if you are late, I will understand."

Damian didn't know how to react when his coach called him Jared's friend. Since the Bell Game, Damian hadn't spoken much to Jared. They'd talk here and there in class, but nothing outside of that.

"So, what's in it for me?" Damian murmured. It was the first question that popped into his head, but once he said it out loud, he realized how selfish it must have sounded.

Coach Jones leaned back in his chair and disappointedly said, "If his grades get better, you will be helping your friend. But, if that's not enough for you, I promise to do a better job of getting you playing time. I won't promise you a starting position or substantial time; you have to earn that. But I will get you in."

Damian stared at his coach for a moment, considering the proposition, then looked at Jared and asked, "Do you want my help?"

Jared looked at Damian with a frustrated stare and said, "We both know I suck at school and that I won't go to college without some scholarship. I can't earn one on the bench. So yes. I want your help if you're willing to," Jared turned away, facing the wall again.

"Great!" Coach Jones said, standing up. "It's a deal then. Well, boys, I wish you luck. Jared, I will check your grades in two weeks. You two have until then to improve your grade. You can start by catching up on Jared's late work." He was smiling in a way Damian thought was fake. "Now get out of here and have a good weekend." He directed them out the door and into the locker room, where they waited for their rides home.

The two friends sat on a bench outside the school in

uncomfortable silence, not daring to look at each other. Jared stared at his scuffed sneakers, and Damian kept shifting, running a hand through his hair. Damien had wanted to offer words of comfort or devise a plan of action, but seeing the mixture of shame and disgust in Jared's gaze quashed that idea quickly.

When Damian saw his mom's car pulling into the parking lot, the two still hadn't spoken a word to each other. As Damian walked from the bench towards his mom, he heard Jared's voice behind him, barely above a whisper: "Can I catch a ride with you? My mom is still working night shifts."

Damian turned and smiled, "Sure, man. No problem." Damian said. "Maybe now they could begin to plan for a study hall?"

"Let's save it for Monday. I can't right now, dude." Jared groaned.

Damian spent the weekend looking for ways to assist his friend. He found various tutorials on the Internet for re-membering facts like historical dates and names and different strategies for understanding English grammar. Surprisingly, he was taken with the prospect of helping his friend learn.

When the final Monday bell sounded, Damian gathered all his items together and walked to the cafeteria for study hall with Theresa by his side. "So, what are you going to do with Jared?" she asked as she followed Damian to study hall. "He's a piece of work, you know. He only focuses on one thing!"

"Girls?"

"Exactly!" They both laughed.

"Well, I think I'm just going to start with his homework, and then we'll try to catch up on his late work. But we'll see." Damian said, remaining upbeat.

Her halfhearted smile conveyed to Damian that it was challenging to help someone who didn't want it. But Damian was determined to do whatever he could for his friend. He wanted him to succeed.

As the two walked side-by-side, Damian often glanced out of the corner of his eye at Theresa. They were standing close together in that hesitant way that high schoolers do when they feel something for each other. Both were beaming, and their arms lightly brushed against one another as they moved forward. It was almost like they held hands, but neither dared to make it official.

"Well, I hope he actually works with you and doesn't sit there while you tell him the answers. Like seriously, don't let him do that," Theresa said after some time walking the halls.

"Don't worry about it," Damian replied. "He'll do his work. I will be his guide now and maybe show him a few things."

"I hope you're right, Damian," Theresa said.

When they showed up at study hall, Damian and his classmates noticed that the old-timer, Mr. Grays, oversaw the session. He was elderly, but his sharp tongue displayed an intelligent wit. Mr. Grays was often in charge of in-school suspensions or after-school student gatherings.

Once, Damian saw a picture of Mr. Grays in a yearbook from the 80s, thirty years ago. He was even teaching back then and had a huge afro. He must have loved teaching to stay around in the same place for so long. He was also hard of hearing, so he often yelled when speaking, and you had to yell back so he'd hear you. He also had many stories about when he was in school. Mr. Grays had a habit of rambling on while telling his stories, as a grandfather might when explaining his childhood to a grandchild.

"Hello, Mr. Grays!" Damian yelled from across the cafeteria. The old man didn't even seem to notice.

"Like I said, good luck. Looks like I'll be walking home alone again today." Theresa said, teasing him as she walked away. Damian thought about saying something cute at that moment, something that might show interest, but decided to reserve his comments for later.

"Hello, Mr. Grays!" Damian tried once again.

This time, he got his attention. "Mr. Frost, what's going on, man? I never thought I'd see you in Study Hall. Aren't your grades good?"

"Yes, but I'm here to help Jared with his homework!" Damian replied.

"Who?" Mr. Grays said.

"Jared Hall!"

"Oh yes, yes, that makes much more sense. That boy's always fooling around. Talking back and messing around on his phone."

Damian nodded in agreement and sat in the front of the classroom against a wall. "Well, I'm hoping I can change that, Mr. Greys! I think he needs someone to push him in the right direction. Do you know what I mean?"

Mr. Grays gave a wry smile and cautioned, "Don't get your hopes up too much. You only get so many opportunities to turn things around for the better. Some learn this lesson after it's too late. When luck comes knocking, grab it and take advantage of what you've been given. Don't let the chance pass you, or you'll be left in the dust."

Damian sat there and smiled awkwardly, thinking about what Mr. Grays meant and wondering why everyone wished him luck today.

Time passed, and Damian began to wonder where Jared was. They had met earlier in class, and Damian reminded him to come to study hall later that day. He knew that it was today. "Maybe he's at his locker or something." He thought.

He began to do his homework to pass the time while waiting for his friend. He started on his math homework first, which was only a ten-question worksheet. He laughed every time he saw his math homework because it was easy, even for a kid who hated math. After finishing the worksheet, Damian looked around for Jared again, hoping to see him walk in, but he was nowhere to be found. "Where is he?" whispered to himself, growing impatient.

A half-hour passed, and Jared still needed to show. Mr. Grays looked at Damian from time to time with sympathy in his eyes. He realized that Jared would show only briefly before Damian had.

Damian felt immense disappointment that Jared had flaked in the study hall, and he sat there in his chair, wondering what to do now. "Should I tell Coach Jones? No, Jared would never speak to me again. Maybe he forgot? No, there's no way I reminded him earlier today. He could have gotten caught up doing something. But that's not a good excuse at all either."

Damian grew angrier the longer he tried to rationalize why Jared was sitting beside him. "I'm trying to help this guy. Why wouldn't he come and show face, at least? It's not like anyone is asking him to be the next Einstein! Just do the bare minimum." Damian was now visibly frustrated, so much so that Mr. Grays took notice.

"I don't think your friend is coming," Mr. Grays said. "I hate it when I'm right sometimes."

"Yeah, and I wish I were right more often," Damian replied,

looking down at his desk.

"What?" Mr. Grays said.

"I said yeah! I'm getting that feeling, too!" Damian repeated frustratingly.

Then, without hesitation, Damian picked up his things and left the room. His practice would start soon, and he had to prepare for it. He walked down the hallway to the auxiliary gym where practice would be held that afternoon.

As he approached the theater adjacent to the auxiliary gym, he heard two voices echoing down the hall. One was a girl's voice, and the other was Jared's. "What the hell!" Damian thought to himself as the anger inside him built up. "How could he blow me off for some girl!" His blood was boiling.

"Oh, stop it, you're too funny, Jared." whispered the female voice suddenly. They were becoming more defined as Damian approached. "You really should be in study hall, though. Damian is going to be upset when he sees you." The girl's voice seemed familiar to Damian for some reason, but she spoke so faintly that he couldn't tell whom it belonged to.

"Don't worry about him. He'd end up doing my work for me anyway. I'd rather you be my study buddy." Jared whispered back.

Now Damian was mad. He began to walk a little faster. With every step, he gradually got more upset. "What an ass!" He mumbled under his breath.

Finally, he was closer now. The voices became more accessible to tell where they were. He realized they were around the corner. "Come on now, don't be like that to him. He's a nice guy." The girl said.

"I'll show you a nice guy," Jared said next. Damian thought about how corny that line sounded.

"Mmm, Jared. We shouldn't. You know how…" The familiar sounds of kissing suppressed her words. And by the sounds of it, the girl did not object.

Damian rounded the corner, prepared to confront Jared for ditching him during study hall, when he halted in his tracks. The girl was Theresa, locked in a deep kiss with Jared, who showed no signs of wanting to let go. Damian's mind raced as he stood there, stunned and unsure what to do next. He had never suspected that Jared had feelings for Theresa. Now, they were locking lips quite passionately, and she seemed to be reciprocating his feelings. They were so engrossed in each other that neither noticed Damian standing a few feet away.

In that instant, Damian's instincts kicked in. Without a word or noise, he turned on his heels and took a different course toward the auxiliary gym. As he walked, his eyes straight ahead, he saw no interaction with any soul he passed by. When he finally arrived at his destination, he let out an exasperated scream and gave one of the tiled walls a hard punch. He was confused and upset about what had occurred, but practice couldn't be over soon enough.

When his teammates arrived, they found him there, clearly unhappy. Michael was the first to ask if he was ok, and Damian responded, "No. But I will be."

That practice was by far the best day of basketball Damian had ever played and the most aggressive. All his shots were on point, he finished in the top three in every sprint, and he even out-hustled Jared on several plays. But to Damian, it was all a blur of anger, and oddly, he found the whole practice therapeutic.

After practice, Damian didn't talk much. Even on the ride home, he was silent. He didn't eat when he got home but walked up to his room and slept—hoping that he'd wake up and everything would be better.

He woke up the next day in a similar mood as when he fell asleep. The anger was gone, but in its absence, self-loathing crept in. He dragged himself out of bed, showered, and made it to class on time. He even avoided Theresa.

Math that day couldn't have been more awkward for him. He walked into class, purposely not looking at anyone, and took his seat as usual. He sat there, waiting for the class period to be over. When the warning bell rang, Damian looked around the room only to find that neither Theresa nor Jared was there. "That's weird. Usually, Theresa is here earlier than me." Damian thought.

Then, a new substitute walked into the class. He was a large, hairy man with dark arm hair and a thick beard. His big, round belly moved side to side as he did. He wore a short-sleeved blue collared shirt and too-small slacks. He looked like a massive blueberry to Damian, and he tried not to laugh at the sight.

The substitute had a messenger bag of papers, which he placed on the desk in separate piles. Once he had organized the stacks of paper, he began to write "Mr. Anderson" on the whiteboard.

The students began to shuffle in faster, but still, Theresa and Jared were nowhere to be seen. Finally, right before the late bell rang, the two of them stepped into class together, holding hands and giggling at one another. They seemed happy together, which only made Damian angry. They both took their seats and exchanged flirtatious gazes at one another.

"Hey, guys. My name is Mr. Anderson," the substitute began. "And I will be your math teacher for the remainder of the year." The class started to murmur frantically as if there was something different about Mr. Anderson than the other substitutes before him.

One student, Thomas, raised his hand and asked, "Um, Mr. Anderson, sir. Aren't you an administrator?"

"Why yes, I am," Mr. Anderson said. I'm currently the senior classes admin, so I wouldn't be surprised if most of you have never met me before, seeing as your freshmen. But I'm also a former eleventh—and twelfth-grade English teacher, and when the school needs a long-term emergency teacher," he smiled, impressed with his importance. Then I'm the one they call."

He began to pass out a worksheet to the class. "I want you all to tell me what you have learned. I realize you haven't been through a lot since Mr. Fritz left, but you should have been taught something now. With only a few days before winter break, we won't get much done right now. But when you come back, we will start fresh again. "

"What happened to Mr. Fritz anyway?" Theresa called out.

"Well, you see. He decided to…"

Damian's attention shifted away from Mr. Anderson as his anger toward his friend and Theresa resurfaced. He was still upset with Jared for dating Theresa, and irrationally, he was also upset at Theresa. His thoughts kept him from truly listening to a word of the teacher's lecture.

"Damian Frost?" Mr. Anderson called out.

"Huh?" Damian said, shaking himself out of his thoughts.

"Are you Damian?"

"Yes?" Damian was perplexed. He missed something obvious.

"Are you present? I'm taking attendance." Mr. Anderson said, staring at him smiling. He was joking. That was apparent.

"Yeah, I'm here."

"Good, try to keep it that way." Mr. Anderson said before continuing his roll call.

Damian, now embarrassed, looked towards Theresa for a comforting expression. Usually, in moments like this, she would give him a look that made him feel better. When he turned and looked at her, though, she was still staring at Jared, indifferent to Damian or what had happened so far in class.

Jared was making funny faces at Theresa, which made her giggle regularly and winking at her. It was that sickening flirtation that young couples exhibited in public settings. They were indeed a couple. That message was loud and clear to Damian. He couldn't get the image of the two of them making out in the halls out of his head, no matter how hard he tried.

"Damian! Turn around. I need you to focus on class soon." Mr. Anderson said.

Again, shocked back to reality, Damian said, "Huh, sorry. I guess I'm out of it today."

"Well, get back into it. Focus on the here and now."

"Yes, sir," Damian said under his breath as he tried to focus on class. He had to take things as they came today and try to get the thought of his two lips-locked friends out of his head.

At the end of another loss the following day, Damian once again shook the other team's hands and prepared for another end-game spiel from Coach Jones. He was out of it today, barely paying attention to the game while on the bench. Even while his coach talked about the game, Damian could not focus.

Damian slammed his locker shut and rolled his eyes. The Jared situation was getting out of hand, and it felt like it was all on him to devise a solution. He flashed back to Theresa – all their conversations, the way she laughed at his jokes, the look in her eyes when he said something clever. He had so many chances to ask her out but never did, and he felt a sinking sensation in his gut; deep down, he knew this was all his fault.

As he packed his locker, ready to leave and begin his winter holiday break, Damian heard his coach call out for him and Jared to enter his office. He knew that this moment would come eventually, where he'd have to sit there and talk about how Jared had blown him off during study hall, but not so soon. As he retook his seat next to Jared, he started to go over what he would say in his head, making sure it made sense before saying it.

"How's study hall going, boys?" Coach Jones asked after shutting the door to his office.

Jared quickly replied, "Great, it's been great. Right, Damian?" He looked at Damian with a large grin.

Damian shifted uncomfortably, his fingers fidgeting as he looked away from the disappointed gaze of his coach. He could feel a lump forming in his throat, and his heart thumped against his ribs as he thought about Jared. He imagined Jared's laughter echoing through the locker room and how he had stood up for Damian on the football field - almost coming to blows with Luke earlier that year. Damian remembered what Jared had said the last time they met: college was his only chance, and Damian knew that if he told the truth right then, it would mean crushing that dream. With a heavy heart, Damian kept quiet.

"Yeah, it's been great." Damian finally said.

"That's great to hear! Jared, just so you know, I've checked back in with your teachers, and it looks like you've been turning in your work. Good start." Coach Jones said, giving a thumbs up to the two of them. "Damian, I want you to keep helping Jared. And I'm a man of my word. You'll see more time as well."

"Thanks," Damian said, not knowing how to feel.

As the two again waited for rides outside the school, Jared thanked Damian for covering for him. "I know I bailed on you, but I have some good news. See, Theresa's been helping me with homework. We don't need to say anything to Coach Jones about that. You can keep getting all the credit. Win-win, right? I seriously appreciate it." Jared said.

"No problem. Theresa is smart. She'll be able to help you, no doubt." Damian said, trying to stay engaged.

"Yeah, listen, I know you had a thing for her, man. I'm sure you think bad of me for claiming her first, but it happened. We talked one day during math, which led to seeing each other for lunch on the weekends. It grew from there. I'm sorry. I should have told you, but it was awkward. You know what I mean?" Jared said, trying to ease what had happened.

"Yeah, I get you. It is what it is. It's my fault for not asking her all this time." Damian said back, not wanting to fight a losing battle.

"Yeah, true. I could hook you up, though, bro. Just let me know, and I'll find you a girl. One that's into linemen and all." Jared said, laughing.

Damian couldn't help but chuckle and reply, "That's ok. I'll take care of myself, thank you very much."

Damian was still upset, but it was getting easier to bear by the minute. He had the entirety of the winter break to relax and regroup after everything that happened this week. As he hopped into his mom's car, he turned to offer a ride to Jared as he had done so before. This time, Jared declined, opting to walk home tonight from school.

As the car left the school, Damian felt comforted that at least he and Jared were again on okay terms. Plus, there was Christmas to look forward to and the new year after that. It was time to recharge and regroup, and Damian planned to do both.

CHAPTER 9 - MR. FROST

"It was amazing, Dad! All the kids did so well!" Damian gushed to his dad as they stepped out into the freezing backyard. Christmas morning brought Damian's family together, and they huddled around a bonfire to keep warm.

Lee and Marie, along with their significant others, were home now. Lee wore an oversized black jacket with an Edgewater County Police bag stitched onto the front. His wife, Gretchen, was close by, huddled up against him to keep warm.

Marie was closest to the fire, wearing a Virginia Tech hoodie that was large enough for her to wrap four times around. It was probably her boyfriend's, and he was helping himself to a cooler of beer. The two had met in college through mutual friends and had been dating for five months. As his family was from France, he couldn't fly home this year, so Marie invited him to join her family celebrations.

Things had changed so much from when they were kids. They used to visit both grandparents on holidays and be with family all winter break. That changed when Damian's grandparents passed away. Ever since then, the family rarely met up with one another. People started to be around their core family instead. Something felt wrong about that to

Damian, though he found it hard to explain.

"All the skits were different, and some were funny because of how dramatic they were. Barrett did well, too, and he even ran his group. Did I tell you he's Michael's nephew?"

His father chuckled, "Yes, you did. I'm glad things went well. You know, you got to let them do their own thing sometimes. Let them decide for themselves and all. It's good for them."

"I wouldn't do that. I know if you had let me do my own thing in high school, I would have talked with friends and shot some hoops," Lee said, joining the conversation and making a basketball-shooting motion with his hands. "Teens got everything but school on their minds."

"Yeah, I hear that. Sometimes, it feels like babysitting, in a way. If I don't structure the day out exactly right, they will stop listening to me or lose focus. There's a give and take, you know?" Damian said, placing his hands near the fire for warmth.

"So, is this babysitting going to get you a job at some point?" Lee said as he leaned back in his chair and sipped beer.

"Hopefully. There's no guarantee, but at the very least, another school might hire me after working as a full-time sub. If not, I don't know what I'll do." Damian said. "I don't plan on living here forever, no offense, Dad."

"None taken. I wouldn't mind some alone time with your mother." His father replied, chuckling. Both Lee and Damian awkwardly laughed along with him, uncomfortably taking another large drink of beer.

"You know," Gretchen said, "We are always looking for new administrative assistants if it doesn't work out. It doesn't pay much, but it's full-time work. We're not federal employees, but maybe it would be a good option for you to start at."

"Really? What would I do?" Damian replied curiously.

"Oh, well, it depends on where you're placed. If placed in the contracting office, you would probably file paperwork and set up meetings and documents. But, if you were placed in building security, you'd be working with people directly on their access cards and whatnot. If that makes sense."

"Seems like it varies quite a bit," Damian said hesitantly.

"You'd be right about that. But I've been doing it with the US Marshals for a few years now. If nothing else, it's a hell of a resume builder." Gretchen said, smiling.

"Not a bad one either," Damian's father interjected. "Plus, it could lead to government work. That's what you need, Damian."

"We're always looking for recruits, too," Lee said, joining the conversation again. "Boot camp sucks, but you'd survive."

Damian stood perplexed, weighing the options before him. He had listened carefully to his mother, who counseled him that all he needed was a college degree, but here he was, having done all the right things to get what he wanted, yet unable to secure a full-time job without proving himself further.

His gaze shifted from one career path to another. Teaching seemed like the most agreeable option, but the thought of working with children, even if it meant succeeding in life's demands, weighed heavily on his shoulders. Perhaps a complete shift in career direction was what he needed—something new and something without the reliance on kids.

Then Damian remembered why he wanted to teach. People like Mr. Anderson and his coaches shaped his viewpoints and led him down the right path. He tried to do the same for another.

"I'll think about it." He finally let out, not denying any

options while not confirming any either.

"Of course. Just let me know." Gretchen said, still smiling.

Just then, the gate to his parents' backyard creaked open, and Michael entered, whom Damian had invited to the family dinner. It was like old times when Michael showed up in time to eat, Damian thought to himself as he waved at his friend.

"Ah, my other son!" Damian's father said, and he stood up to greet Michael alongside Damian's mother.

"It's great to see both of you. Did all of you get shorter?" Michael replied mockingly.

"Shut up, Michael!" Damian's mother said jokingly as the rest of the group laughed.

"Well, looks like we have to head out, guys," Lee said, finishing his beer and taking Gretchen by the hand.

"So soon?" His mother replied.

"Yeah, I need to be on my shift early tomorrow morning. I want to get some shuteye before then. It was good seeing you, Michael."

As the night drew on, the fire embers glowed like a million little eyes watching them. Marie and her boyfriend giggled as they retreated inside; Damian's parents soon followed suit, leaving only Damian and Michael under the stars with their beers in hand.

They reminisced about their wild youth, swapping tales of misadventure and adolescent mischief while crickets chirped in the background. The memories were bittersweet; life had been easy then, but now everything felt uncertain.

Suddenly, Michael's face fell into a solemn expression. "I have something to tell you, "He declared, eyes locking onto Damian's. "I invited Jared over."

Damian choked on his beer and began to cough. "What!"

he struggled to say as he tried to catch his breath. It had been years since they'd seen each other, and though he talked about catching up with him to Michael, he never expected it to happen so soon.

"I know it's late, but he was in town and hit me up," Michael replied. "I thought, hey, why not? No time like the present."

"No, I want to see him," Damian said finally. He was being honest; he did want to see his old friend. The uncertainty came from how they interacted. "How did he sound?"

"Same as always," Michael answered. "A ball of energy. My throats are a little raspy now, though. I'm pretty sure he's the same person we knew growing up."

"You think he will be high when he shows up? He was the last time."

Michael shrugged his shoulders, "I'm not sure. We'll see."

"Yeah," Damian said. "We will see."

Marie appeared through the home's door and called out to the two friends. "Hey guys, we're headed out. It was nice seeing you again, Michael. Don't be a stranger."

"I won't. Get back to school safely and tell your new boyfriend it was nice seeing him, " Michael said, laughing.

Marie smiled and shook her head, then waved goodbye. Damian thought about how old everyone was now. It didn't seem all that long ago that they were all still in school together. Time seemed to slip away like a flash of light, and it wasn't stopping soon.

Damian and Michael continued to feed the fire, adding wood and sending plumes of smoke into the night sky. Damian's parents retreated inside to sleep off their wine buzz, leaving the boys alone with the flames. If things were tense between them and Jared, at least they had privacy.

At last, Jared strolled through the gate, his palm raised in greeting. He wore a light blue shirt decorated with a lime green bird and ripped jeans that looked like something one of Damian's students would wear.

"Nice shirt," Damian said, offering a tentative smile.

Jared shrugged, "Thanks." But his face belied the coolness of his response.

The air between them was tense as they settled onto plastic chairs around the fire. The flames danced between them as though they were waiting for someone to make a move.

Though his loosely fitted clothes were those of a young person, Jared's physical appearance was aged beyond his years. His lanky frame was still recognizable but had become gaunt and stooped with age. His once glossy black hair had begun to dull. Deep wrinkles creased his forehead and bracketed the sides of his mouth. His skin had lost its youthful glow, and he now sported an uneven beard and longer shoulder-length hair.

"Damian! How the hell are you!" Jared said as he made eye contact.

"What's going on, man," Damian replied as the two hugged. Jared squeezed Damian much harder than he expected, nearly causing him to cough. "You were never this strong," Damian struggled to say.

"Yeah. You have to love the gym, man. Plus, working at the University of Richmond gives me free access. Oh, and then there are the ladies and drinks." Jared seemed to be the only one to laugh at that joke.

"What do you do at the university?" Michael asked.

"Recreational Engineer," Jared said with a smile on his face. "or more commonly known as a janitor. Hey, it's a good living."

"That is great! You have to love work perks. Glad to see that you made it up here in one piece." Michael said encouragingly.

Damian was glad to see that Jared was able to keep a job. When he was in high school, he had a habit of taking on part-time positions at the mall. He began working immediately and usually stayed employed for six months or less.

One time, Jared was working at Footlocker as a shoe salesman. Initially, this suited him fine since he got discounts on new shoes. After some time, though, Jared started giving his discounts away to anyone who came by the store, which didn't sit well with management, resulting in his dismissal.

Then, there was a time he worked at a kiosk in the mall, fixing phones and selling phone cases. Again, it was a great job at first. He got all the new cases and customized his phone with ease. But he quickly got bored with it and started showing up late or not at all. It wasn't long before they fired him as well. Still, Damian was happy to hear that his friend had a stable job.

"Grab a seat, man," Damian said, unfolding a fold-out chair and placing it beside him. "Want a beer?"

"No, I'm good. I don't drink." Jared said, waving off the question and grabbing his seat. "Haven't had a drink for some time now. Just smoking weed for me, haha." He laughed as he pulled a joint out of his jacket packet. "But you all go ahead. Don't stop because of me."

Damian tossed his empty can aside, grabbed another, and said, "So smoking's cool, but not beer?" He chuckled to lighten the mood of the statement.

"Man, alcohol doesn't hit the same, you know what I mean?" Jared said with a slight smile. "It's all fine, but the comedown is brutal if you don't watch it." Damian felt himself about to rebut but stopped himself from doing so.

Michael then jokingly reached over and punched Jared in the shoulder like they were kids. They laughed and talked about football like schoolboys, argued about who the better athlete was, and made fun of each other for the silly things they did in high school. It was just like old times.

After a few laughs, Jared looked around the yard, seemingly looking for something missing. Then, he looked back at his friends and said, "I wonder what Theresa's been up to?" Damian choked a little on his beer. "She's the only one missing from all this. The four of us used to be inseparable."

"No idea," Michael replied. "It must have been five years since I've heard her name. Damian, do you have any idea?"

Damian had tried to keep in contact with Theresa, even though he hadn't heard from her in a while. He sent her messages periodically but rarely received replies. In school, friends always seem to be around; you don't think about losing touch with them. But once graduation passes and everyone starts living their own lives, relationships can lapse easily for years at a time. This was what happened with Damian and Theresa.

Damian recalled their unexpected encounter at the grocery store. He was there to pick up some items for his mom when, out of the corner of his eye, he spotted Theresa in the cereal aisle. As soon as Damian saw her, she noticed him, too. They locked eyes for a few seconds before walking towards each other and embracing. At that moment, they talked and planned to meet again later that week, but it never happened.

"It's been a while since we've talked," Damian said after some time in his thoughts. "Jared, she was your ex-girlfriend. If anyone knew what she's been up to, it would be you."

"Man," Jared sucked in air between his teeth. "That's your girl, remember? We didn't even last two months." He said, laughing.

"Not my girl. We never went out." Damian snapped, remembering that day after study hall suddenly.

"Let's not bring up old flames," Michael said, dismissing the topic altogether. "How long are you in town, Jared?"

"I'll be heading back tomorrow. Got to get back on schedule at the school. Used all my PTO just to be here a few days to see y'all."

"Well, keep in touch. You always have us up here if you need anything." Damian said.

"I know. Honestly, I moved down there so as not to be lonely, with some buddies from school while they were in college. But now, everyone's moved on, and I feel so isolated sometimes, if that makes sense. Some nights," Jared paused, struggling to explain, "It's just a lot. You probably don't understand, but it is. Day after day, doing the same thing over and over. Work, eat, sleep. It makes me want to drink again, though I know better." Jared said, exhaling as if he was disappointed in himself.

"We get it, man," Michael said. You keep doing what you must, making that money. We both want to see you happy and hopefully, you know we're always here for you."

"Yeah, Jared, we're only a call away if you need anything. It's a short drive to Richmond." Damian said.

"Thanks, I do miss you guys," Jared said, lifting his water bottle, "A toast. To reunite and bring the boys back together."

Damian and Michael raised their bottles and said, "Cheers."

It was a pleasant moment in Damian's mind. Jared appeared to have gotten his life back on track, whatever that entailed precisely. The rest of the vacation benefitted him as he could move away from school and think about matters differently. He just had to get through one more month, and then he would be free to begin applying for open positions next year. For once, all seemed orderly as he watched the embers slowly die out.

CHAPTER 10 - DAMIAN

amian's winter break was off to a delightful start as he embarked on his journey between his grandparents' houses for Christmas. He spent the first few days mostly in bed, wearing sweatpants and playing video games. He hadn't realized how much gaming time he missed, with football and basketball occupying his time.

Today, however, was different because it was Christmas, Damian's favorite holiday. The smell of freshly baked cookies and ham wafted through the house as he went downstairs to join the bustling chaos of his extended family. He loved them all, even if they could sometimes be a bit overwhelming. With a smile on his face, Damian embraced the holiday spirit and looked forward to spending quality time with his loved ones.

As the car rolled into the quaint town nestled in the Shenandoah Valley, Damian's eyes lit up at the sight of snow-covered mountain tops and the promise of a winter wonderland. His grandma Martha's cozy home was tucked away on a quiet street. The perimeter of the home was adorned with white Christmas lights, and a wreath on the front door contained a verse from the Bible.

The moment he stepped inside, he was welcomed by the comforting scent of snickerdoodle cookies baking in the oven and a pot of rich hot cocoa and mulled wine simmering on the stove. The crackling fire in the fireplace created a warm and inviting atmosphere that made him feel like he had entered a Christmas movie. Family photographs and festive decorations adorned the walls, while the familiar sounds of laughter and a Christmas parade playing on TV filled the air.

With her flour-dusted apron and kind smile, Grandma Martha greeted him with open arms. She may not have been the best cook, but she always had plenty of sweet treats for her grandkids. As Damian settled into a comfortable armchair by the fire, he couldn't help but feel grateful for this special place that his mother had grown up in and now shared with her family every holiday season.

With a gentle tug, Grandma Martha removed her flour-dusted apron and set it aside. She emerged from the kitchen carrying a golden, steaming apple pie. The scent of cinnamon and nutmeg filled the room as she put it on the dining table. Not wanting to miss a piece of hot pie, Damian got up, sat at the table, and cut a slice. Memories flooded his mind as he savored each bite, the flaky crust melting in his mouth. He looked around the cozy living room, lit by a crackling fireplace, and felt grateful to be surrounded by loved ones during the holidays.

Damian's fork clinked against the empty plate that once held a slice of warm pie. He looked up from his spot at the dinner table and took in the scene before him. His parents' voices mingled with Grandma Martha's high-pitched laugh as they sat together on the plush couch, drinking and chatting about old memories. The crackling fire in the fireplace cast flickering shadows on their faces, highlighting each furrow of joy and love etched into their expressions.

In the corner of the room, nestled in the armchair he once sat, slept Marie curled up in a ball. It was midday during a holiday, and she was still tired. Her small body rose and fell with each breath as she basked in the warmth radiating from the fire. Their grandmother's scruffy dog lay by her feet, content and snoozing—two peas in a pod.

On the other side of the living room, Uncle Jake and Aunt Emily were deep in a game of charades, accompanied by Lee and their cousins, eagerly guessing their clues. Damian couldn't help but smile at their close bond despite the chaos and noise filling the room. For now, it was nice to be surrounded by family, even if it was a bit louder than Damian preferred.

The room was a vision of festive delight. Cascading strands of shimmering tinsel adorned the walls, creating a sparkling backdrop for the celebration. In one corner stood a regal Christmas tree, towering above them all, its branches heavy with twinkling lights and an enchanting array of ornaments collected over the years. Each ornament seemed to hold its special meaning and memory, making the tree seem alive with stories and nostalgia. As Damian gazed upon it, he couldn't help but feel like the tree held all his hopes and dreams for this holiday season, not to mention the presents stacked neatly beneath it.

The clock hands ticked closer to noon, and the family gathered around the Christmas tree, excitement building in Damian's chest. His sister handed out gifts with a mischievous grin, and soon, wrapping paper was flying everywhere as they tore into their presents—the room filled with laughter and shouts of joy as each gift was revealed. Grandma Martha clutched a new cookbook with her treasured dessert recipes close to her chest while Lee's face lit up at seeing a brand-new pair of basketball shoes. Uncle Jake's eyes widened when he unwrapped a new fishing rod, and Aunt Emily couldn't stop smiling as she admired her delicate sparkling necklace.

Damian's heart raced as he watched the pile of presents under the tree slowly dwindle. When his turn finally arrived, he carefully chose a small package with a shiny gold bow. His name was written neatly on a tiny tag.

He tore off the wrapping paper with trembling hands to reveal a stack of old hardcover books. The musty smell of aged pages filled his senses, and he couldn't resist running his fingers over the worn spines. As he read each title, a sense of wonder and excitement grew.

Despite never mentioning his love for reading to anyone, the books before him felt they were chosen specifically for him. They were a collection of classic adventure stories - tales of pirates, explorers, and enchanted lands. He lost himself in the vibrant covers, oblivious to his family's chatter.

"These belonged to your grandfather," Grandma Martha said, her voice filled with a hint of yesteryear. "He used to read them to me when we were young, and I thought it was time for you to have them."

As Damian flipped through the old, worn books, he could almost feel his grandfather's presence. The musty smell of the pages and the familiar handwriting brought a sense of connection to his family's past. His parents had always told him what an amazing person his grandfather was, but now, as he held these treasured books, he could see it for himself. He felt grateful to have this piece of his family's history and couldn't wait to dive into the stories within.

"Thank you so much, Grandma," he said, his voice filled

with genuine appreciation. As they said their goodbyes and headed towards the door, Damian's family gathered their new gifts and piled into the car for one final stop on their holiday adventure.

Their next stop was Pops' house, his grandfather on his father's side. As they pulled up to the impressive brick exterior of the suburban home, Damian couldn't help but feel small compared to its grandeur. The white columns seemed to reach the sky, and as he entered through the tall front doors, he was struck by the coldness of the interior. It was vastly different from his cozy Grandma Martha's house, but Damian felt comfort and belonging in this familiar place.

As Damian stepped inside, he was immediately taken aback by the formal atmosphere. The rich scent of mahogany and leather filled his nostrils, with a hint of cigar smoke lingering in the air. Antiques adorned the walls, including paintings and old black-and-white photos that transported him to a bygone era. It felt like stepping into a different world altogether. He couldn't help but wonder how his father, who was always carefree and happy-go-lucky, grew up in such an environment. He remembered when his grandfather called his father a hippy, to which his father replied with a smile, "That sounds about right, Dad. And I'm a happy one at that."

Pops sat in his favorite armchair, the leather worn and creased from years of use. Wisps of cigar smoke swirled around him as he gestured for Damian to come closer.

As Damian approached, he couldn't help but feel reverence for the man before him. Pops was a pillar of strength and wisdom, his presence commanding respect.

Settling into the chair across from Pops, Damian couldn't help but feel exposed under the weight of Pops' piercing gaze.

He wondered if Pops could see through all his defenses and secrets.

But then, as if to break the tension, Pops reached over to the side table and picked up a small, elegantly wrapped box. The gold paper sparkled in the firelight, and the red velvet bow seemed to beckon him closer. On the tag, Damian saw his name written in Pops' neat handwriting. It simply read, "To Damian, from Pops."

"How's school going, boy?" Pops grunted. The sound stole Damian's attention away from the gift.

"Good, it's going. Not much to report so far. You know me, I'm on the straight and narrow." Damian smiled, hoping to receive one in return but knowing he would not.

"Good, let's keep it that way." He set his cigar down on the ashtray near him. "Your education is important; you don't have to be told that. Your father and your brother had to be told over and over. But not you. You're a smart one, just like me." Damian shifted uncomfortably in his chair at the comparison. "Well, why don't you fetch this old man a drink? See that table over there? Grab a glass, fill it about one-third the way up with that bourbon, and add one of those sphere ice cubes from the freezer for me.

Damian nodded obediently, rising from his seat to fetch Pops his drink. As he moved across the room to the small bar area, he couldn't help but feel a sense of heaviness in the air. It was always this way when he visited Pops – a mixture of admiration and apprehension that lingered like a thick fog.

The crystal glasses shimmered under the warm light of the chandelier as Damian carefully selected one. He poured the right amount of bourbon, watching it swirl gently with the large ice cube at its center. His hands shook slightly as he returned to Pops, silently handing him the drink and avoiding eye contact. A heavy silence hung between them as Damian waited for Pops' reaction.

Pops accepted the glass with a nod of approval and took a sip, his gaze fixed on Damian, who once again took his seat. "You're getting taller every time I see you. Before long, you'll be towering over me," he remarked gruffly.

Damian chuckled softly, sensing an unspoken challenge in Pops' words. "I doubt I'll ever be as tall as you, Pops." He was tall when he wasn't seated squarely in his leather chair—the only man of height on either side of Damian's family. Everyone else was average to slightly above average.

Pops leaned back in his worn armchair, a wry grin on his face as he watched Damian's reaction. His gruff voice softened with emotion, and a glint of pride shone in his eyes as he spoke. "You may never reach my height, but you have your strengths, boy. Intelligence, curiosity, and a strong moral compass. Those will take you far in life," he said.

Damian felt a surge of warmth and gratitude at his grandfather's words. Pops rarely gave compliments, but each one meant the world to him. He shifted in his seat, suddenly aware of the weight of the wrapped box between them.

"Oh, I almost forgot," Pops continued. "I have something for you." He gestured towards the small box on the coffee table with a weathered hand. The gold signet ring on his pinky finger glinted in the sunlight streaming through the window.

Curiosity mingled with apprehension as Damian reached for the gift. The wrapping paper crinkled beneath his touch as he carefully peeled it away, revealing a wooden box underneath. The box was a large dice with a hinged door at the top. Opening the door, the words "Liars Dice" were engraved underneath, along with a small sheet of rules, six small dice, and three small cups bound in leather.

Damian's eyes widened in surprise as he took in the box's contents. He had heard of the game of Liars Dice from old movies but had never played it before.

Pops watched him closely, a knowing shine in his eye. "This box specifically has been in our family for generations since we came over on wooden ships," he rumbled, his words heavy with significance. "It's a test of wit and strategy, not for the faint-hearted or dumb."

Damian nodded, his fingers tracing the engraved words on the box lid. As Damian listened to Pops' words, he felt a sense of responsibility settle over him. This was more than a gift; it was a legacy, a connection to his ancestors and the generations before him. He could almost feel their presence in the room, guiding his hand as he reached for one of the dice.

Damian exhaled deeply and lifted his gaze to meet Pops' stern but loving eyes. Damian rose from his chair and embraced his grandfather tightly, shining determination in his own. The awkwardness between them was palpable, but Damian didn't care.

"Thank you, Pops," he said, his voice trembling with emotion.

Pops grumbled in response, trying to maintain his tough exterior. He cleared his throat gruffly, and a faint blush tinged his weathered cheeks. But the twinkle in his eye gave away his true feelings.

"Don't go getting all soft on me now, boy," he said sternly, but the corners of his mouth quirked up in a small smile.

Damian chuckled at Pops' attempt to downplay the sentimental moment and settled back into his seat by the crackling fireplace.

As the crackling fire filled the room with warmth, Pops leaned back in his chair, and Damian did the same. They sat there for some time in silence, watching the flames flicker and quietly listening to the conversations around them.

Damian's fingers twitched with anticipation as he clutched the game box in his lap, feeling the smooth cardboard and intricate illustrations under his palms. He couldn't wait to test his skills and outsmart his opponents, just like Pops had taught him.

As the night wore on and the guests said their goodbyes, Damian could barely contain his excitement. He furtively looked at the game box in his lap, its edges illuminated by passing streetlights outside.

When they were driving home, his father noticed Damian's intense focus on the box. "You really can't wait to play, can you?" His father chuckled, catching Damian's eye in the rearview mirror.

Damian nodded eagerly, his eyes sparkling with anticipation. "Yeah, Pops surprised me with this one. I can't wait to learn to play Liar Dice and continue the family tradition."

His father chuckled, glancing back at Damian with a fond smile. "Family tradition? No, son. I was there when Pops bought it many years ago at an antique shop in the city. It's just an old game, not some family relic." His father's laughter filled the car, a warm and familiar sound that wrapped around everyone like water in a pool.

Damian's heart sank as the realization hit him like a ton of bricks. The sentimental attachment he had formed to the game shattered instantly, leaving a hollow feeling in his chest. The words "family tradition" echoed in his mind, mocking him with their false significance.

He slumped in his seat, arms crossed tightly over his chest. His eyes were fixed on the passing landscape outside, but he didn't seem to be seeing it. The streetlights blurred into a hazy streak of light as they drove by, mirroring the whirlwind of emotions churning inside Damian. He was lost in thought, completely silent for the rest of the car ride.

By the time they arrived home, Damian had tucked the box of Liars Dice away in the corner of his room, the large letter mocking him. The books he placed gently on his desk, taking care not to bend or ruin them in any way.

As the night grew more profound, and the world outside his window fell into a blanket of darkness, Damian could not shake off the disappointment that had settled in his heart. The glow of the streetlights filtered through the curtains, casting a soft luminescence on the wooden box that sat alone in the shadows.

He lay awake in bed, tossing and turning as the frigid winter air seeped in through the old window of his room. Despite his restlessness, he took comfort in knowing he still had a few days left of winter break to relax before returning to the daily grind of school.

CHAPTER 11 – MR. FROST

Damian sunk into the soft cushions of his couch, the TV flickering before him. A rerun of a trashy reality show filled the screen. He half-heartedly watched as couples argued and made poor life decisions, the perfect distraction from tomorrow's return to his substitute teaching job. But as he watched, his mind drifted back to a conversation with Michael and Jared not too long ago. The warmth and camaraderie between them filled him with a sense of the good old days, but he couldn't shake off his concern for Jared's difficult circumstances, something not unfamiliar to him.

Damian's phone chimed with a new email as the opening theme music played. He pulled it out and saw it was from Mrs. Martinez, who also cc'd Mr. Anderson. The subject line caught his attention: "End on a High Note." With a mix of curiosity and concern, he tapped on the email and read a heartfelt message from Mrs. Martinez.

"Dear Damian," the email began, "I wanted to take a moment to express my gratitude for your hard work and dedication during your time as my substitute teacher. I know it can be difficult to handle all the work of one handling the classes and two juggling the teaching and grading of assignments. Your efforts have not gone unnoticed, and I believe you have positively impacted our students."

"So far, so good," Damian thought before reading the email.

"As we enter the last month of your time with the class, I want to ensure that a few things are done before I return. First, please ensure all assignments you give are graded before I return. It will be challenging for me just entering the class to grade them, and even more difficult for you to come in and finish. Second, ensure all computers and school properties are returned to the front desk and IT folks. And finally, please make sure all your items are taken with you out of the classroom on your final day."

Damian grabbed a pen and notebook not far from him, realizing it would be best to write these instructions down and add them to his calendar later.

"I have heard that some classes have given you trouble. Mr. Anderson has kept me up to date with everything. I thought your last-minute assignment before winter break was creative." the email read. Damian wanted to be happy at the comment but was wary. "But that being said, please stick to the assignments I've laid out for you. I realize you were in a pinch to get scores up, and I appreciate the effort, but our lesson plans are the way they are for a reason."

Damian felt the criticism like a knife to the gut. That was nicely said, but the message was clear to him and having Mr. Anderson copied on the email only twisted the dagger more.

"I know this was your first time taking over multiple classes over a long span of time, and I hope you learned a lot about the craft of teaching in doing so. Of course, please make sure to leave your substitute information on my desk on your last day. I would love to call you in on short notice if I need you. Best of luck moving forward, and again, I'm here if you have questions." The email concluded.

The email from Mrs. Martinez sat in Damian's inbox, taunting him. He couldn't shake off the mixture of anxiety and frustration that had settled in his gut. Had he been blind to some crucial element of teaching? Was his college education needed to prepare him for this job? As he half-heartedly watched a reality show on the TV, his mind was consumed by memories of his failures in the classroom.

He remembered the time he struggled to keep a rowdy group of high schoolers focused during a lesson on Shakespeare. Their eyes glazed over at the mention of iambic pentameter, their restless energy palpable. Damian had tried every trick in the book to engage them, but it felt like he was fighting a losing battle. Mrs. Martinez echoed in his mind, urging him to reflect on his teaching methods.

With a sigh, Damian set aside his phone and notebook, his thoughts consumed by self-doubt. Maybe he wasn't cut out for this after all. Perhaps his passion for teaching wasn't enough to overcome the challenges he faced in the classroom. The weight of Mrs. Martinez's expectations bore down on him, suffocating any enthusiasm he had left. Damian's mind raced with self-critical thoughts as the reality show blared in the background.

Just then, keys jingling at the front door interrupted Damian's spiraling thoughts. He looked up to see his father entering the home, a mischievous glint in his eyes.

"Well, well, well," Damian's father boomed with a grin as he tossed his keys onto the side table. "If it isn't my middle child, all grown up and still lounging on the couch. Should I also fetch you a refreshing beverage?"

Damian smiled weakly at his father's teasing tone, grateful

for the distraction from his overwhelming thoughts. His father had a knack for bringing a sense of levity, even during the most somber moments. Whether he realized it or not is another question.

"I'll take a cold one if you're offering," Damian chuckled. He pointed one finger in the air as if he were calling for a waiter at a fancy restaurant.

As they settled down in the living room, Damian's father at in his chair and examined his son's face. "So, what's got you looking like a lost puppy, son? Trouble at work?"

Damian hesitated momentarily before opening to his father about the email he had received from Mrs. Martinez. He recounted the contents of the message, and the weight of each word seemed heavier as he said them out loud.

His father listened intently, nodding as Damian shared his doubts and frustrations about his teaching abilities. When Damian finished speaking, there was a moment of silence between them as the words hung in the air.

Then, to Damian's surprise, his father laughed heartily. "Is that all that's been bothering you?" he exclaimed, slapping his knee for emphasis. "Son, let me tell you something. Teaching is a tough gig, no doubt about it. But you've got the heart for it. I've seen how you light up when you talk about literature and genuinely care about your students. You may stumble, but that's all part of life's journey. You learn from your failures and become a better teacher because of them."

Damian leaned back on the couch, absorbing every word his father spoke. He could feel a sense of calm wash over him, like a weighted blanket covering his body. As his father's words sank in, Damian realized the depth of his unwavering support.

"Thanks, Dad," Damian said. "I needed to hear that."

His father winked at him before raising the leg rest on his chair. "Now, enough moping around. Let's order some pizza and watch one of these bowl games. Your favorite meat lovers, just like old times?"

Damian's father's suggestion brought a hesitant smile to his face. He constantly faced challenges and obstacles as a teacher, but his family was always there to support him. Yet, he couldn't shake the doubt and uncertainty, making it hard to feel genuinely optimistic or determined.

The two happily devoured slices of greasy pizza while watching a football game on the screen. As Damian observed the players fighting for victory on the field, his mind raced about the parallels between their struggles and his battles.

The words of his sister-in-law persisted in his mind like a persistent echo. She had mentioned a government contracting job opening that she thought would be perfect for him. The idea had seemed far-fetched at first, but now, in the dimly lit room surrounded by the familiar scent of pepperoni and melted cheese, it took root in Damian's consciousness.

"Dad," Damian began, his voice sounding unsteady, "What if I decide to go another direction, one away from teaching? Is that waste at this point? I mean, Gretchen mentioned the whole government contracting thing. Maybe I'd be a better fit there. I'm not sure, honestly."

His father thought momentarily, answering, "Well, I wouldn't make any big decisions right now. You got a weird email, but that doesn't mean you need to pivot. Let's finish this job and see if you can get a full-time position next school year. There's no rush, so don't feel like you need to be in a hurry."

"You're probably right. I need to see how things play out."

"Exactly," Damian's father said before finishing his beer.

Damian lay in the quiet of his childhood bedroom later that night, contemplating his options. He imagined didn't scenarios for his life as if staring into the multi-verse of his timeline. In one world, he's a principal walking the halls of some future school, giving students high-fives and stern looks. In another, he's giving a presentation on a topic he doesn't understand, but judging from the crowd in his head, it goes well.

He would have continued traveling these timelines until his eyelids became heavy if not for the sudden vibration of his phone beside him.

Jostled from his thoughts, he sat up and stared at the phone, silencing the vibration. On the screen, he saw Jared's name in bold letters, accompanied by a photo of the two of them younger and smiling at the camera. Damian couldn't remember the last time he'd received a call from Jared. His heart raced with surprise and apprehension as he answered the call.

"Hello," Damian answered cautiously, unsure what to expect from this unexpected contact.

"Hey, man, it's Jared!" His voice sounded unusually chipper on the other end of the line. "I was just sitting here watching TV and thought, 'I wonder what Damian's up to on a Sunday night?' How are things?"

Damian hesitated momentarily, "I've been… alright," he replied faintly. "What about you? How's everything on your end down in Richmond?"

"Things are good, man, things are good," Jared replied, his voice colored with a hint of unease that Damian couldn't quite place. "I wanted to give you a call because, well, I've been thinking about our friendship a lot recently." As Jared continued, Damian could hear the nervous shuffling of papers in the background. "You know I've always valued it, and I'm glad we could all meet up earlier. I missed hanging out with you both, man. Remember all that trouble we used to get into back in high school?" He laughed, and Damian dimly did as well.

Damian felt a sense of foreboding settled in the pit of his stomach. He had a sinking feeling about where this conversation might be leading.

"Well, I won't beat around the bush," Jared said finally, his tone shifting as he composed himself. "I'm in a bit of a tight spot financially right now. Things have been rough with work, and now my rent is due, and I was wondering if you could help me out just this once."

Damian felt emotions swirling as Jared's words hung in the air. He could sense the desperation in Jared's voice, mingling with a touch of shame that prickled Damian's empathy. However, he also remembered all his past experiences helping Jared out and where that led them.

He remembered how that story ended when he agreed to his coach's request to help Jared in study hall. He remembered taking him to work and picking him up when he would be let go for whatever reason. But he remembered the heart-to-heart conversations they'd had walking home from practice and all the summer nights he'd stay over because he was arguing with his parents.

"I… I understand things must be tough right now," Damian began carefully, choosing his words cautiously. "But I need to think about it. How much are we talking? I don't want to commit if I can't help."

Jared fell silent on the other end of the line, and the air

suddenly became thicker.

"Damian, come on," Jared's voice was strained, desperation creeping into his tone. I wouldn't be asking if I didn't really need this help. You know I'd do the same for you in a heartbeat." The words he spoke were laced with memories of their past, familiar-sounding and tugging at Damian's emotions.

As Jared begged for understanding, Damian couldn't help but feel the heavy pressure of their friendship resting on his decision. He knew Jared had always been one to push boundaries with their friendship, but this request seemed different somehow. Damian hesitated, unsure of how to balance his loyalty with his self-preservation. The flicker of doubt in his mind grew as he tried to navigate the conflicting desires.

"I know, Jared, I know," Damian replied quietly, running a hand through his hair as he thought. "But this is a big ask, and I need time to process everything. Can I sleep on it?" His voice held a note of finality, a silent plea for understanding.

There was a pause again, "Sure, man, that's fine. Just let me know." The conversation ended there before each said their farewells ended the call.

That night, Damian tossed and turned in bed, his mind consumed by the weight of Jared's request. The shadows danced across the ceiling, casting eerie shapes that seemed to mirror the uncertainty in Damian's heart. Memories from their past, the good and the bad.

As dawn broke, Damian found himself no closer to a decision. The morning sunlight failed to chase away the shadows that lingered in his mind, casting a pall over his breakfast and following him into his lunch hour. Damian couldn't shake off the heaviness that clung to him throughout the day, his thoughts consumed by Jared's plea for help. The image of Jared's strained face, the desperation in his voice, replayed in Damian's mind like a broken record.

He decided to put the issue to rest. He had the money; other than his experience with him as a kid, he had no reason not to help a friend. He messaged Jared, sending him the money through Venmo, before brushing the crumbs off his shirt and preparing for his next class period.

CHAPTER 12 – DAMIAN

Damian lay in bed, the winter chill seeping through the old window and biting at his skin. He pulled the covers tighter, a smile spreading across his face as he recalled his grandparents' laughter and the cozy evenings they spent together. The soft glow of streetlights cast shadows that danced on the walls. He knew sleep wouldn't come quickly, but there was one thing he was looking forward to spending time with his brother, Lee.

The following day, the sun peeked through the curtains, casting a warm glow across Damian's room. He rubbed his eyes and stretched, the cold air stiffening his movements. He glanced at the box of Liars Dice, still sitting in the corner, and sighed. He shook off the lingering disappointment and focused on the day ahead. Lee had promised to play basketball with him, which was always something to look forward to.

The smell of breakfast greeted him downstairs, and he followed the scent to the kitchen. Lee was already there, flipping pancakes with ease. His muscular frame moved with a fluid grace, a testament to his athletic prowess.

"Morning, sleepyhead," Lee flashed a warm smile, his eyes crinkling at the corners. "Pancakes are almost ready. You hungry?"

"Starving," Damian replied, sliding into a chair at the kitchen table. "Thanks for making breakfast."

Lee shrugged, the corners of his mouth quivering in a grin. "No problem. Figured we could use some fuel before hitting the court."

They ate in companionable silence. The only sounds were the clink of cutlery and the sizzle of pancakes on the griddle. The warm, sweet aroma filled the kitchen, watering Damian's mouth. He took a bite of the fluffy, golden pancakes, savoring the buttery sweetness that melted in his mouth—a perfect start to the day.

After breakfast, they bundled up in warm clothes and headed outside. The crisp winter air bit at their cheeks, but the sun shone brightly, casting long shadows across the driveway. The basketball court was a short walk away, and they made their way there, the crunch of snow underfoot the only sound.

The court was empty. The lines faded but were still visible. Lee dribbled the ball with ease, the sound echoing in the stillness. Damian watched his brother, admiring his skill. Lee's movements were fluid and confident, and each ball bounce was controlled and precise.

"Ready to play?" Lee asked, tossing the ball to Damian.

Damian caught it clumsily, his fingers cold and stiff. "Yeah, let's do this."

They started with some basic drills, Lee patiently guiding Damian through each one. His voice was calm and encouraging, offering tips and corrections without making Damian feel incompetent.

"Keep your knees bent," Lee advised, dropping into a low stance, his movements fluid. "It'll help you stay balanced and move faster."

Damian mimicked his brother's stance, adjusting his position until Lee nodded in approval. They continued with dribbling drills, Lee's movements a blur of speed and precision. Damian tried to keep up, his breath coming in puffs of white in the cold air.

"You're getting better," Lee said, clapping Damian on the shoulder. "Just keep practicing."

After an hour, they took a break, sitting on the edge of the court. Lee pulled out a water bottle and handed it to Damian, who took a grateful sip. The water was cold and refreshing, a welcome relief after the exertion.

They resumed their practice, the ball bouncing on the pavement, filling the air. Lee showed Damian how to shoot. Damian's shots were less accurate than Lee's, but he did his best to keep up.

"Focus on your form," Lee instructed. "Don't worry about making the shot every time. Keep practicing, and it'll come."

Damian nodded, concentrating on his technique. He bent his knees, positioned his hands on the ball, and aimed. The ball arced through the air, hitting the rim and bouncing off. Damian groaned in frustration, kicking at the snow.

Lee retrieved the ball and handed it back with an encouraging smile. "You're getting there," he said. "It's all about practice."

They played for hours, the cold air invigorating and the exercise warming their bodies. The sun climbed higher in the sky, casting long shadows across the court. They laughed and joked, their bond growing stronger with each passing moment.

As noon approached, they decided to take a lunch break. They walked back home, the smell of grilled cheese sandwiches wafting from the kitchen. Their mother greeted them with a smile, her cheeks flushed from the stove's warmth.

"How's the game going?" she asked, setting plates on the table.

"Great," Lee replied, giving her a quick hug. "We're working up quite an appetite."

Damian nodded in agreement, his stomach rumbling at the sight of the sandwiches. They ate quickly, the food disappearing in a matter of minutes. The warm, gooey cheese and crispy bread were the perfect comfort food, filling them up and giving them the energy to continue their practice.

After lunch, they headed back to the court. The afternoon sun cast a warm glow, and the shadows lengthened. Lee suggested a one-on-one game, a chance for Damian to put his skills to the test.

"Ready to take me on?" Lee asked, a competitive glint in his eye.

Damian grinned, feeling a surge of determination. "Bring it on."

They played intensely, Lee's skill and experience evident in every move. He was faster and more robust, his shots precise and his defense impenetrable. But Damian held his own, using Lee's teaching techniques and giving it his all.

Lee scored the first few points quickly, and his movements blurred with speed and agility. But Damian quickly adapted, learning from his brother's moves and finding ways to counter them. He scored a few points, each a small victory that boosted his confidence.

"Nice shot," Lee said, clapping Damian on the back.

"Thanks," Damian panted, his breath coming in short gasps. "I'm getting better, right?"

"Definitely," Lee replied, his smile genuine.

They continued playing, the friendly competition pushing them both to their limits. Lee's encouragement and support were constant, and his advice helped Damian improve with each game. They took breaks in between, sitting on the edge of the court and catching their breath.

"You know, I'm going to miss this," Lee said, his voice tinged with a hint of sadness as they rested on the court's edge.

"Miss what?" Damian asked, looking at his brother curiously.

"Playing with you, hanging out like this," Lee replied, a note of sadness in his voice. "I'll be heading off to college soon, and things will be different."

Damian felt a pang of sadness at the thought of his brother leaving. "Yeah, I guess they will. But you'll come back, right? We can still play during breaks and holidays."

"Of course," Lee said, ruffling Damian's hair. " "We'll always have time for this," Lee assured, ruffling Damian's hair. "And who knows, maybe you'll be better than me by then."

Damian laughed, the idea of surpassing his brother seeming impossible but exciting. "I'll hold you to that."

As the afternoon turned into evening, they decided to head back home. The sky was painted with hues of orange and pink, and the setting sun cast a warm glow over everything. They walked in companionable silence, feeling their bond grow stronger.

Back home, they were greeted by the comforting smell of dinner cooking. Their father was stirring a pot of stew in the kitchen while their mother set the table. The warmth and coziness of the house contrasted with the cold outside, creating a deeply comforting sense of home.

They ate dinner together, and the conversation flowed easily. Mary chattered about all the exciting things she'd done with her friends over the holidays. Lee shared stories about his college plans, and his excitement was evident in every word. Damian listened intently, feeling pride and sadness. He was happy for his brother but knew he would miss him terribly.

After dinner, they settled in the living room, the fireplace crackling and filling the room with warmth. Damian felt content, and the day's activities left him pleasantly tired. He glanced at Lee, sitting next to him, a sense of gratitude washing over him.

"Thanks for today, Lee," Damian said softly. "I had a great time."

"Me too, little brother," Lee replied, his voice equally soft. "We'll do it again soon, I promise."

The night grew more profound, and the family members retired to their rooms one by one. Damian lay in bed, the day's events replaying in his mind. He felt a sense of peace, the previous night's disappointment fading away.

CHAPTER 13 – MR. FROST

Damian adjusted the rearview mirror as he glanced at the passing scenery. The streets were illuminated with the soft glow of streetlights, and the occasional flurry of snowflakes danced through the air. Michael was fiddling with his phone in the backseat, but Damian focused on the road ahead and the company beside him.

"Man, I'm looking forward to this game," Lee said, rubbing his hands together. His excitement was palpable despite the car heater's struggle against the bitter cold. "It's been too long since we went out like this."

Damian nodded, a small smile tugging at his lips. "Yeah, for real. Life's been hectic."

Lee leaned back, his Edgewater County Police jacket making a slight rustling sound. "Tell me about it. Between work and Gretchen, I barely have time to breathe."

Michael chimed in from the backseat, not wanting to be left out of the conversation. "Well, at least you have someone to share that time with. All I've got is a TV remote and a couch."

Damian chuckled. "You'll find someone, Michael. Need to stop scaring them off with your police stories."

Lee laughed, shaking his head. As the car turned a corner, the bar appeared, its neon sign glowing brightly against the night sky.

Stepping out of the car, the cold air hit them like a wave. Damian zipped up his jacket while Lee pulled his beanie further down over his ears. Michael, ever the tough guy, pretended not to notice the chill.

The bar was warm and inviting, nothing like the cold air outside. The scent of fried food and the hum of conversation filled the air. The brothers and Michael found a booth near a large TV screen showing pre-game commentary. The murmur of excited patrons created a lively atmosphere.

Lee took off his jacket, revealing a simple flannel shirt underneath. "I'll get the first round. What's everyone having?"

"I'll take a beer," Damian said, sliding into the booth. "Nothing too heavy."

"Same here," Michael added, his eyes already glued to the TV screen.

Lee made his way to the bar, easing through the crowd. Damian watched him momentarily, a sense of pride welling up inside. His brother had always been the dependable one who looked out for everyone. Now, as an officer, he seemed to carry that responsibility with even more gravitas.

"Here we go," Lee announced, setting three pints of beer on the table with a satisfying clink. "To a good game and even better company."

They raised their glasses in toast, and the cold beer was a welcome contrast to the bar's warmth.

"So, how's work been, Lee?" Damian asked, genuinely curious.

"Busy," Lee replied, taking a sip of his beer. "You wouldn't believe some of the things people get up to. But it's rewarding, you know? I feel like I'm making a difference."

Damian nodded. "Yeah, I get that. Teaching can be like that too, in its way."

Michael interjected, "I don't know how you both do it. Dealing with people all day? I'd go nuts."

Lee laughed, shaking his head. "It's not for everyone, that's for sure."

The conversation flowed naturally, shifting from work to childhood memories. With each passing minute, Damian relaxed more, the stresses of his job and uncertainties about the future fading into the background.

The game started, and the bar erupted in cheers. Lee and Damian focused on the screen, the intensity of the match pulling them in. They discussed plays, argued over calls, and celebrated every touchdown with high-fives. Although less invested in the game, Michael joined in with the enthusiasm, his comments often sparking laughter.

As the first half of the game progressed, the three ordered more drinks and a platter of appetizers. The bar's atmosphere grew more animated, and the excitement was contagious. Damian found himself lost in the camaraderie.

During a commercial break, Lee leaned in closer, his expression more serious. "Damian, I've been thinking about what you said the other day. About finding a full-time job."

Damian met his brother's gaze, his curiosity piqued. "Yeah?"

Lee nodded. "I want you to know that I'm here for you whatever you decide. Whether it's teaching, something in the government, or even if you want to join the force. I've got your back."

The sincerity in Lee's voice touched Damian. He knew his brother meant every word. "Thanks, Lee. That means a lot."

They clinked their glasses together again, silently promising support and solidarity. The game resumed, and they returned to their lively banter and cheering.

As the night wore on, the bar began to thin out, but the energy at their table remained high. The game was close, and every play had them on the edge of their seats. Lee's enthusiasm was infectious, and Damian couldn't help but get caught up in the excitement.

"Man, this game is nuts!" Damian exclaimed with his eyes glued to the screen. "I can't believe that last play."

Lee grinned, his eyes twinkling with excitement. "I know. This is what football is all about."

Michael, who had been relatively quiet, suddenly jumped up, pointing at the screen. "Did you see that? Unbelievable!"

The brothers laughed, sharing their joy at the moment. They finished their beers, ordered another round, and continued to immerse themselves in the game.

Eventually, the game ended, the final score sparking a wave of cheers and groans from the patrons. Damian and Lee high-fived, their team having come out on top.

"That was one for the books," Lee said, his voice hoarse from all the cheering.

"Definitely," Damian agreed, feeling a sense of contentment wash over him. "We should do this more often."

Lee nodded, his smile reflecting Damian's sentiments. "Absolutely. Life's too short not to make time for this."

As they prepared to leave, Michael excused himself to the restroom, leaving the brothers alone momentarily.

"Hey, Damian," Lee said, his tone more serious now. "I know things have been tough for you lately. But you're going to figure it out. You've always been the smart one in the family."He then took the final gulp of beer from his glass, and set it on the bar top.

Damian looked at his brother, appreciating the words of encouragement. "Thanks, Lee. That means a lot coming from you."

Lee clapped him on the shoulder. "Remember, no matter what, we've got each other's backs."

Michael returned, and they settled the bill, leaving a generous tip for the bartender. As they stepped back into the cold night, the camaraderie and warmth of the evening lingered.

The drive back was filled with laughter and conversation. The brothers and Michael reminisced about the night's events. They delved into the past, sharing stories and memories that were dear and fun.

"Remember when we tried to sneak into that game at Jefferson High?" Lee said with a mischievous grin on his face.

"Oh man, that was a disaster," Damian laughed. "We got caught before we even made it to the gate."

Michael chuckled from the backseat. "And who was the genius who thought climbing the fence was a good idea?"

"Guilty," Lee admitted, raising his hand. "But hey, it was worth a shot."

"Thanks for tonight, Lee," Damian said as they stepped out of the car.

"Anytime, little brother," Lee replied, pulling him into a hug. "We'll do it again soon."

As they parted ways for the night, Damian felt a warmth that had nothing to do with the bar or the heater in the car. It was the warmth of knowing he had a brother who would always be there for him, no matter what. And as he headed to bed, he knew that whatever the circumstances might ever be, he wouldn't have to face it alone.

CHAPTER 14 - DAMIAN

Damian's return to school after break was slow. His science teacher gave worksheets with pictures of dinosaurs and instructions to color them. His English teacher, Ms. Grey, put on a movie about a family of bears and told everyone to look for the symbolism. Now and then, one of Damian's teachers would explain how they were all suffering from "Winter Break Brain"—an imaginary illness that made it hard to focus until they got back into their routine again.

It was the last period of the day, and Damian found himself in his history class watching a movie on Napoléon and the French Revolution. Ms. Stone was feeling the effects of "Winter Break Brain," which meant that Damian had to pay enough attention to answer the questions on the worksheet she provided for the class.

As the last few minutes approached, students gathered around the door, ready to leave. Even though Ms. Stone always protested this behavior, students lined up, ready to exit. It wasn't hard to understand why they did; Ms. Stone was closer in age to Damian's classmates than any other teacher at the school, making it difficult for her to gain credibility.

A sudden knock on the door caught Ms. Stone's attention.

Upon opening it, a note carrier from the office handed her a pink slip to pass to one of her pupils—Damian. A pink slip was a notice to meet with someone following the final bell, and Damian eagerly read who had summoned him after school. It was Mr. Anderson, his still new math teacher. "What did he want?" Damian thoughtfully wondered.

The bell signaling the end of recess was the only thing Damian heard as he rushed to his math classroom. As he entered, he spotted Mr. Anderson sitting at the desk, eyes scanning a stack of papers—most likely grading them. Suddenly, Damian's stomach twisted into knots. To him, it felt like Mr. Anderson was a dictator ready to deliver out punishments.

"Come in, Damian. Grab a seat." Mr. Anderson finally said in a tone that only heightened Damien's nervousness. He approached the desk and took a seat in front of his teacher. Mr. Anderson still looked through his papers, acting as if Damian hadn't entered the room.

"So, I see that you've been distracted in class. Want to explain?" Mr. Anderson said. He did not look up from his papers.

"Uh, yeah, I've been a little distracted. It's girl stuff, not a big deal." Damian said nervously, laughing and waving off any concerns for it.

"Girls, you say. Well, that makes sense, I suppose." Damian didn't know how to respond to that. "It's that, Theresa, isn't it?"

Damian felt the color rush from his face as the questions bounced around Damian's head. How did anyone know? Was it written on his face? Had he been too obvious? He opened his mouth to speak but could only get one word out: "How...did you know?"

"Damian, you keep staring at her in class. And you look at her boyfriend, too; what's his name… Jared. I'm guessing you missed your window, am I right?"

"Yeah, but I'm ok now. I had to get over it. The break helped." Damian said with a tinge of melancholy in his voice.

Mr. Anderson slowly set his scattered stack of papers on the table and finally glanced up at Damian, squinting in concentration as he analyzed the young man's face. His brows softened as a wave of understanding swept over him, and his stern expression melted into one of sympathy. "Kid, I'm going to give you some advice. There are four things you don't wait for in this world." He held up four fingers. "They are planes, trains, taxis, and girls. There's always another one coming, eventually."

Damian nodded, taking in every word Mr. Anderson had said. They floated around in Damian's head. He knew that Mr. Anderson was correct; other girls were out there.

"Now, I called you here for another reason. Your grades are slipping, Damian. Right now, you have a C- and based on the grades you've been getting on quizzes, you'll likely end up with a D by the end of the quarter. I need you to focus more on yourself, Damian. You understand?"

Damian saw his new teacher's eyes filled with concern. "I'll do better, sir." He finally made himself say.

"Good. I'll make a deal with you. If you can get a B this quarter, I'll bump it up to a B+. Sounds good? It won't be easy, but it'll be our secret."

That made Damian happy. "Sounds good." Mr. Anderson extended his arm, and Damian clasped it with a firm handshake. With the deal sealed, Damian quickly stood up and bowed slightly to Mr. Anderson before departing the room. His mind was now set on his task and determined to get that B.

Damian stumbled into the locker room, glancing around as he made his way to his locker. Michael and Jared were seated together, though both were lost in their world, until Damian's gaze met Jared's. Suddenly, an awkward tension in the air seemed to spread through the entire room.

"How was the break, guys?" Damian said, attempting to break the ice.

"It sucked…" Jared said in a frustrated tone. "My dad is back in town. Tried to act like everything was cool with us." Damian tried to say something to console Jared but was quickly cut off. "Then, Theresa got upset over break because I didn't get her a gift. Like, we started dating only a few weeks ago. I'm not thinking about all that. The break was so whack, like I said."

"I'm sorry to hear that, man." Damian managed to say finally. Jared said nothing in return. Frustratedly, he grabbed his practice jersey and left Damian and Michael behind.

Practice was hard that day. They spent more time running sprints and shooting free throws than practicing their plays. The JV season was ending, and Damian's coach wanted to guarantee the team was in shape.

Their coach also wanted to show his players what was expected at the next level, which was only going to be more challenging next year. It wasn't easy, and after practice was over, Damian could barely walk straight.

"If you'd just made those two free throws, we would have finished earlier," Jared said to Michael as the team gathered in the locker room. "Damn, practice sucked!"

"Hey, I was tired. And besides, you missed foul shots, bro."

Michael snapped back.

"Yeah. But mine came after we ran extra suicides because neither of you made your shots." Damian kept his head down, avoiding the conversation altogether.

Jared was right though. Both Damian and Michael were terrible from the free-throw line that day. Damian was usually sure-fire about making his free throws. It was about the only sure-fire thing he could do on the court other than play defense and foul. Today, though, he was not on point. The break must have taken a lot out of him.

"Whatever, it's over. Do better next time and stop complaining." Michael said to Jared.

The three friends left the locker room, the cold January air filling their lungs with a crisp chill. As they waited in the school parking lot for their rides home, the distinct sound of a diesel engine hummed in the distance. Michael's father pulled into the lot, his green truck standing out among the other cars. The loud crackling of its engine reverberated through the air like thunder. Michael smiled as he hopped into the cab, leaving Jared and Damian alone in the silent darkness.

Some time passed, and neither of the boys' rides showed up. As Damian grew impatient, his mother texted him, asking if he could walk home tonight. She was caught up in a parent meeting with Marie and didn't know when she'd be able to pick him up.

"Sucks for you!" Jared said jokingly.

"Eh, it's okay. It happens. Luckily, neither of us live too far away. Maybe I'll walk out these sprints," Damian replied. "Want to come with me?"

After being asked, Jared looked around for a while, then shrugged his shoulders and said, "Sure, why not? I'll text my mom."

The two began their walk home, their feet crunching on the gravel road and the golden light of the setting sun streaming through trees lined on both sides of the street. The sky was a spectacular display of oranges and pinks, and as they walked, clouds glowed in shades of orange, yellow, and red.

As they crossed a street, Jared asked, "So, how do you feel on the bench? You know, there's no way I could do that every game. No way."

"It's not that bad. If I don't play, it's whatever. I mean, I want to, so don't get me wrong. But basketball is a good workout during the off-season." Damian said, smirking, trying to reassure himself more than anything.

"True, I guess. I was thinking about doing track in the spring season. I'll work on my speed for football. You think I could start next season?" Jared said, taking a bag of chips out of his backpack. He opened them, then asked, "Want some?"

"Sure," Damian answered, reaching into the bag and grabbing a handful of chips. "We were weak in the secondary. You get fast enough and can cover well enough; you'll be the starter."

"Yeah, I hear you. You'll be starting for sure. I mean, you got out there this year and played well."

"I suppose so. The line had a lot of injuries, though. I'm not going to give up that starting spot easily, but starting as a freshman means the pressure is on me moving forward." Damian spoke with conviction in his voice. He often felt the need to perform well; it wasn't only because he started as a freshman or because Lee did it as a freshman. It was a desire within him to be successful and make the people who loved him proud. He couldn't bear the thought of letting them down.

"You know, it's not often that an opportunity flies right at you where you can catch it. But, when fortune knocks, you must answer its call." Jared said, jarring Damian out of his thoughts. "You'll be fine, Damian; take advantage of the opportunity."

"Thanks, man. When did you get all philosophical?" Damian chuckled.

"Nah, it's something my grandma said once." The two of them laughed at the thought.

Damian and Jared slowly returned to his house as the evening grew darker. He noticed that his mother's vehicle had yet to be returned home. Turning to Jared, he offered, "Do you want to stay here for the night? We don't have school or anything else tomorrow."

"Nah, not tonight. I should try to stay home more often. But if I change my mind, I'll let you know." Jared answered. He waved goodbye and turned down the street towards his block.

Damian watched Jared meander down the street and turn left, ensuring his buddy was headed in the right direction. He figured it would be good if Jared tried to stay in his house more often and get along with his family. It may not have been ideal, but at the time, he felt that avoiding them wouldn't solve anything.

Damian opened the door to find his father sitting in his recliner chair, eyes fixed on the golf match playing on the screen. A can of beer rested between his legs. Damian made his way over to the couch and sunk into the cushions. His muscles relaxed as he watched, feeling familiar comfort wash over him.

"How was practice? The season's coming to an end now." Damian's father asked.

"Yeah, hard one today. Is Mom still at that parent meeting?

Must be important for her to be over there so long."

"Yup, I'm not sure what it's all for—probably trying to do a bake sale to raise money. Do you remember when we made brownies to sell when you were in middle school? I think it was for a trip to DC or something like that." His father drank his beer, seeming to empty the bottle.

"Oh yeah, I remember that. We went to all the museums downtown that day." Damian recalled the day very well. It was a fun day in the city with his schoolmates, though they were stuck like glue together in groups.

"I ordered pizza if you're hungry. I didn't know how long your mother would be, so I figured I'd order something." Damian's father pulled back the leg rest in his recliner, stood up, and started walking toward the kitchen. "You want a slice?"

"Sure, thanks, Dad," Damian replied as his father left the room. The moment he was alone, a peaceful quiet settled in the air. He slowly laid back on the couch and closed his eyes. The darkness of his inner world slowly began to unravel before him. In the distance, he could see another figure—a boy about his age—but he couldn't reveal any facial features or details. Suddenly, in the far corner of this dark space, a large red door appeared out of nowhere with a deep rumbling sound in its wake—a continuous loud knocking emitted from its center.

Damian's adrenaline surged as the figure beside him took off towards the door. He dashed forward, pushing his legs faster and faster, desperate to catch up. However, no matter how hard he ran, a gap between them still seemed unbridgeable.

With one final burst of energy, the figure reached the door first and yanked it open, vanishing outside instantly. Damian stumbled to a stop, lungs burning with exhaustion - in time to hear keys rattling in the lock behind him and the creak of someone entering his home.

He stirred from his sleep and rubbed his eyes. His mother and sister stepped in apprehensively, Marie hurrying to her room without a word. His mother stood there momentarily; her shoulders slumped like an invisible weight.

Damian's dad walked back into the living room carrying a cold beer and a pizza slice on a thin paper plate. "How did it go at the school tonight?" he asked his wife.

"Just great," she replied sarcastically. "Your daughter volunteered me for the bake sale for this year's field trip. It looks like they're going to Six Flags over in Maryland."

The father smiled over at Damian, then said knowingly, "Called it."

CHAPTER 15 - MR. FROST

With every tick of the clock, Damian's substitute teaching position drew closer to its inevitable end. The sun climbed higher in the sky, casting a warm glow on the bustling school campus. As he walked through the hallways, greeting each office assistant with his usual cheerful hello, he couldn't help but feel a sense of melancholy. Sipping on the last dregs of cold coffee from his morning commute, Damian made his way to the classroom where students were already filtering in, unaware that this was his final day as their teacher. But for him, it felt like any other regular day - a bittersweet blend of routine and farewell.

The calendar pages turned quickly, and before he knew it, January was gone. Despite using Mrs. Martinez's pre-made lesson plans, his students seemed as distracted as he was. Some even returned late from their winter vacations, making catching them up challenging. As February approached, he felt the pressure build as the actual teacher's return loomed.

Though he had no activities planned, Damian ensured that his departure day would run smoothly. First, he told each of his classes that this was his last day with them before surprising them with a grammar quiz to get the ball rolling. He hoped the activity would take up at least 20 minutes.

He'd treat them to a little game at the end of class. Using questions related to everything they'd learned, he'd host a jeopardy-style quiz. It was fun to summarize the material before handing the reins back to Mrs. Martinez.

The students in Damian's classes all responded differently to the news. His morning classes seemed unfazed, especially the class right before lunch. "Maybe they were too exhausted or hungry to be bothered," Damian thought. However, his first-afternoon class was visibly saddened by the news of it being over. But once they heard about the upcoming game they would play, their mood quickly shifted, and the previous news didn't seem as significant.

Damian had grown used to the short attention spans of high school students. It was not a big deal if an event did not directly involve them. They might be upset to see a substitute teacher leaving, but at least they got a game day out of it. All in all, it wasn't so bad from that perspective.

At last, Damian saw his pupils enter the class and take their seats as usual. Unfortunately, they didn't know this was his final lesson before leaving. Once everyone settled down, Damian stood at the front of the class like he usually did when the bell rang.

"Hey, guys. I hope you all are doing well this Friday afternoon. I have a quick quiz for you all to take. It should be easy. But first," Damian stopped as his students began to groan.

"You didn't say anything about a quiz in the last class today?" One student whined from the back of the room.

"I know, I know. But that's why it's called a pop quiz." Damian jokes. The class groaned louder. "Now, now come one. It's not a big deal. You'll live, plus after you're done, we're going to."

Damian stopped once again as the door opened. It was Barrett, late for class again. "Sorry, Mr. Frost. I lost my way. Why the long faces?"

"He's giving us another quiz." A student called out.

Barrett, looking confused, turned to Damian and said, "What, another one? How many are we going to take this year?"

Damian found himself a little embarrassed. He didn't know what to say to calm the class down. "Um, guys, seriously, it'll be easy. Look, it's only like six questions." He turned to pick up the stack of quizzes he had made earlier in the morning and saw that he was short about five quizzes. "Crap." He said a little too loud.

"What?" Barrett replied.

"I've got to make some copies. Hang here quick, everyone. I promise we're going to do something fun after," Damian said as he ran out of the room.

He sprinted down the hall, his breath coming in short gasps as he berated himself for being so careless on his last day. Finally, he reached the copy room and frantically shoved papers into the machine, grateful that it was functional today. He made multiple copies, triple-checking each, then returned to the classroom where he had left his students anxiously waiting.

Damian's heart raced as he approached the classroom door. It was closed, which was unusual since he always left it open for students to come in before him. He searched his pockets frantically but couldn't find the key the school had give him. His anxiety rose as he feared being locked out of the classroom.

He reached for the doorknob with shaky hands, but it wouldn't budge. Through the frosted glass window, he could see his students gathered inside, boisterous laughter and playful banter echoing through the room. He could see them pointing and giggling at his feeble attempts to gain access.

Red crept up his neck and face. He clenched his fists, feeling the heat of anger rise within him. A few students began to lean against the door in defiance. He pounded on the door and shouted, "Open the door now!" Nothing changed. He pounded on the door again, his knuckles turning white with frustration as he yelled for them to open it. But they laughed and shrugged, mocking him without fear. The intense emotion overwhelmed Damian as he realized that even after all this time, these kids still showed him no respect.

"The nerve of these brats!" Damian thought to himself. He could feel his heart rate growing faster and faster. Then, without a second thought, he lifted his arm and slammed his fist into the door. "Open the door, now!" Damian said louder than before. The sound of his voice echoed, this time, down the halls.

The students froze, their eyes wide with fear as they saw the angry red mark on Damian's knuckles from where he had punched the door in frustration. All thoughts of this being a fun, one-sided joke disappeared from their expressions. A tense silence enveloped the room, and even the usual sounds of chatter from other classrooms seemed to disappear. One brave student slowly stood up and cautiously approached the door, opening it to reveal a hallway filled with confused and curious faces.

The students sat in their chairs with nervous expressions, as if they were all afraid of the same thing. Damian stared at them, noticing how tense the room felt, and realized he may have taken things too far. Even Barrett was shocked by his behavior.

Summoning up his courage, Damian walked towards the front of the class with a stack of papers. Still angry, he took a deep breath and said, "We're going to take this quiz now – only six simple questions. It shouldn't be too challenging for any of you."

The class was dead silent as Damian spoke. He could still feel his heart beating heavily in his chest, though by now, it was coming down. He continued, "We were going to play Jeopardy today—a nice and easy day. But no, that was too much for you all. We're going to sit in silence."

There was no arguing, no groans, or questions. He could tell that most of the class was mad, while the rest were sad that they missed out on a game day. The students all sat silently, most having a book open and pretending to read it. That was fine as far as Damian cared now. He watched as the clock slowly ticked away. With only a few minutes left in his final class, he stood up and met all his students' eyes.

"Start packing your things. Today is my last day. In the next period, Mrs. Martinez will be back. And yes, she will know about today." The class began to whisper amongst themselves. "Please, treat her with more respect than was given today." The bell rang almost on cue with Damian's words.

Those were the last words Damian uttered to the class before they got up and packed their things. None of them stayed behind to say goodbye, leading Damian to believe they were too ashamed or even angry with him for making them stay silent.

Only Damian was left in the room as he tidied his desk, making it look nice for Mrs. Martinez to take over next week. He wiped off the whiteboard, threw away any litter, and finally arranged the classroom back to its original setup–desks in a boring manner. Still, it didn't matter since he wasn't the instructor here anymore.

As his last act before leaving, he flipped the lights off. At the front office, he handed in his substitute pass and any property that belonged to the school and offered a fond farewell to all the teachers he had worked with.

Mr. Anderson stood at the front entrance as Damian approached. "How was the last day?"

"As smooth as it could be, I suppose." Damian lied.

"Thank you so much for helping us out. I hope you know we appreciate it." They exchanged a handshake, and Mr. Anderson said, "Keep in touch. There may be an opening for an English teaching job for next year—keep your eyes peeled for the listing."

Damian conjured up a smile and said, "Thank you, sir. You'll hear from me when it is."

When Damian arrived home from school, his father was waiting in the doorway as usual. He asked, "So, how was your last day?"

Damian's throat tightened as he thought of his last day at the school. He remembered the shocked faces of some of his students when he announced that he was leaving and the disaster of a class at the end of the day. He tried not to overthink about it. "Sad. A messy day," he said instead. He plastered on a fake grin and told himself he could find another teaching job anywhere and would never have to face those disappointed stares again. "I'll miss some kids, but what a mess with the rest. Glad to be done with them."

"Yeah, I figured you would feel that way. You put a lot into each of them, hoping they learn from your teaching. But I'm sure they've appreciated it in their way." Damian's father said with a smile. "You never know the impact a little kindness and care can bring."

Damian nodded slowly, feeling the words settle on him like a shroud.

A week had passed as Damian sat on his couch, hunched over his laptop with a tiny flicker of hope. He constantly refreshed the county job site, knowing nothing new would pop up but still clinging to the possibility. His social media feeds were stagnant, filled with familiar faces and mundane updates. In this monotonous routine, he tried to distract himself from the long wait for a job opportunity. As he repeatedly clicked the refresh button, Damian's heart skipped a beat when he saw a new post from Jared.

With eager anticipation, he clicked on his friend's story. It was a short video of Jared sitting at a fancy restaurant with his mother, another person he hadn't seen in years. But now that Jared was back in town, Damian decided to give him a call. After all, they both had some free time to catch up.

As the phone rang on the other end, Damian felt a thrill of excitement course through him at the thought of talking to his friend again after so long. Finally, he heard a click on the line as someone answered.

"Hey man," Jared said into the phone.

Damian responded, "Hey! I was thinking about you recently. How have you been?" he asked inquisitively.

"Good, good! Just hanging out here at home mostly," Jared replied.

Damian could hear the television in the background, and he could picture Jared lounging on his couch with a bag of chips.

"I finished my last day of substitute teaching," Damian said, a sense of disappointment creeping into his voice.

"Ah?" Jared responded. "How was it?"

Damian hesitated for a moment before replying. "It was… mixed. Some kids were great, but others were completely disrespectful and didn't care about anything I had to say."

Jared chuckled. "Sounds like high school to me."

Damian rolled his eyes, but he couldn't help but smile. It was good to hear Jared's voice again.

"So, what have you been up to?" Damian asked, hoping to change the subject.

"Not much," Jared said. "I'm trying to get into some new hobbies, you know? I've been thinking about maybe trying out painting or something."

Damian raised an eyebrow. "You?"

Jared laughed. "Yeah, I know, it sounds crazy. But I figured I should try something new that I've never done before. Maybe I'll surprise myself."

Damian couldn't help but feel a surge of pride for his friend. "That's awesome, man. I think it's great that you're trying out new things. Who knows, maybe you'll be the next Picasso."

Jared chuckled. "I highly doubt that, but thanks for the encouragement. I need something to keep my mind off stuff and keep me on the right path. So, what about you? What's next for you now that you're done with teaching?"

Damian hesitated for a moment, unsure of what to say. "I don't know yet. I'm thinking of maybe taking some time off to figure out what I want to do next."

Jared sounded surprised. "Really? I thought you loved teaching."

"I did; I mean, I do," Damian said. "But after the way things ended at that school, I don't know if I'm all in anymore. It takes so much out of you. But you do have summers off."

Jared paused for a moment before responding. "Well, maybe it's just that school. Maybe you need to find a different one, with students who are more respectful and appreciative of what you do."

Damian thought about Jared's words for a moment. Maybe he was right. Perhaps he needed to find a new school with students more willing to learn and listen to him.

"You know what, you're right," Damian said finally. "I shouldn't let one bad experience ruin teaching for me. I'll start looking for another school, maybe something different this time. Maybe I'll find a place where I fit in better."

Jared sounded pleased. "That's the spirit! I know you'll find something great, man. You're a great teacher; any school would be lucky to have you."

Damian felt his chest swell with pride at Jared's words. It was good to have a friend who believed in him. He knew he needed to take some time for himself, but the thought of finding a new school made him feel more optimistic about the future.

As they continued to talk, Damian realized how much he had missed talking to Jared. He hadn't realized it before, but their conversations made him feel better, no matter what was happening in his life.

Damian couldn't help but feel grateful for his friend as they hung up the phone.

CHAPTER 16 - DAMIAN

Michael's eyes widened as he accepted the wax paper-wrapped sandwich from Damian's outstretched hand. Damian's mother had made it for him the night before, promising to after his last visit. He took a big bite of the turkey, tomato, lettuce, and cheese, with his eyes rolling back in exaggerated euphoria.

"This is delicious. Tell your Mom I said thank you," he remarked before wiping away crumbs from his mouth. "Hey, have you finished that English homework yet? Our baseball game went into extra innings, so I didn't even get to start it."

Sitting in the cafeteria, Damian and Michael were again two friends down. Theresa had been sitting with a different group of friends since the breakup, and Jared was stuck in I.S.S. for wandering the hallways during class too often.

With only two months left until the end of the year, every class was beginning to wind down. As each week passed, Damian found himself doing less and less homework. He would find himself bored at home, but he had decided not to do a Spring sport this year. The only time he felt true joy anymore was on his weight room days with the football team, though they left him sorer than ever.

"Yeah, here it is. It's easy, I just had to skim the chapter for keywords," Damian said as he passed the worksheet to his friend. "How's baseball going? The season is almost over now, right?"

"It's going. You know me, I'm doing my thing," Michael said with a cocky grin, "But, you know, we can't win a game to save our lives." His grin had faded, and he looked disappointed at how things had gone.

"Ah well, there are always other options for you, like summer ball and the travel team. Not to mention, one of the private schools may even come steal you from us," Damian declared, trying to comfort his friend. Michael was highly talented at baseball and had already broken two school records this season; he'd stolen more bases and created more double plays than anyone before him—and he hadn't even finished his freshman year yet. It wasn't his fault the rest of the team couldn't keep up with him.

Michael laughed, seemingly to himself, and said, "Well, maybe, but then it'll become a chore instead of fun. We suck, don't get me wrong, but it is fun playing ball here and hanging out with you and Jared. If I'm at a different school, I don't know. Something tells me we won't see each other as much."

"Nah, man, come on, you'd still live right behind me. My family's not going anywhere," Damian responded,

"Yeah, I guess you're right about that. I'd still be stopping by for more sandwiches like these," Michael said as they both laughed and pounded fists.

Damian arrived at his last class after separating from Michael at the bell. As she had been lately, Ms. Stone was already there, typing away on her laptop fervently. None of them were sure what she was writing, but it must have been crucial.

A mound of paper was placed near the front of the classroom for everyone to pick up. It was another activity, this time focusing on the Peloponnesian War with a picture of Greek warriors engaging in combat. Damian grabbed his worksheet and seated himself, ready for the bell to ring.

When the time came, Ms. Stone called out to the class, "Everyone, please take a seat. You all should have grabbed a worksheet as you entered. We will watch a short film on the Peloponnesian War in preparation for your final for the last quarter. Quiet down! The rest of the class is yours once the movie is finished and your worksheet is complete. Can someone please get the lights to please?"

Her eyes never left the laptop's bright screen as her fingers flew across the keys. Every few seconds, she muttered a command, her words barely audible above the constant tapping of her fingers. Without looking up or slowing down, she used one hand to switch on the TV and press play.

Damian absentmindedly filled in the circles on the worksheet, already familiar with the answers. His teacher must have known that no one was paying attention at this point of the semester, and even if they were, it wouldn't be challenging to pass the quiz. As his pen scrawled across the paper, Damian glanced up at the TV. The drone of white noise from the television set blended in with his thoughts, which had wandered toward daydreams of summer. Pool parties, sleepovers with friends, hours spent gaming—all these joyful scenes played out in his mind like a movie.

Things had changed quite a bit over the past few months; Jared was lost in his world, and Theresa's attention seemed to shift to her other friends, leaving Michael as his only real friend. As Damian pondered these shifts in dynamics, a knock at the classroom door drew the collective attention of both students and Ms. Stone. He watched with curiosity as a small girl with bright red hair entered the room, her arms crossed tightly across her chest, her eyes wide with anxiety. She held up a hall pass that trembled in her hands, and her voice shook as she spoke. "Uh, excuse me. I have a pass for Damian Frost from Mr. Uh, Coach Dean."

"Thank you, Damian, hand over your sheet. I'll find you later to finish."

Damian smiled as he stood up. "I've been done for a while with this. Got to love the History Channel." He kept his smirk as he handed over the worksheet and left the classroom.

When he arrived, the coach's office door was already open. Damian stepped inside and found himself staring up at a figure wearing an orange hoodie and navy blue hat. What were they doing here? Why had Coach Dean invited someone else into the office? The man stood up imposingly as Damian entered, and for a moment, he felt trapped between them.

"Damian!" Coach Dean said, "Thanks for coming. Let me introduce you to Coach Willis from Gettysburg College." As Coach Dean spoke, Damian stepped forward and shook hands with the tall man. Coach Willis gripped Damian's hand and squeezed harder than anyone had before.

"Nice to meet you son." Coach Willis said. He held his hand towards an empty chair, non-verbally directing Damian to sit. "Coach Deans told me a lot about you. You're young, but we like connecting with potential talent."

"You see Damian," Coach Dean introduced, "Coach Willis is only in town this week and asked to speak with players who could be a good fit at Gettysburg. Your name came to mind." Damian, at a loss for words, nodded his head and smiled.

Coach Willis said, "Yes, so let me tell you about Gettysburg College and our program. Then I can answer any questions you have. Here, take a pamphlet," Damian nodded again, now intensely focusing on what Coach Willis said. He looked down at the pamphlet and saw a large capital G on the front, colored half orange and half navy blue, alongside images of players playing in the same colors. "So, to start, we're a division 3 program, which means…"

Damian thumbed through the glossy brochure, glancing up every few seconds at the imposing figure of Coach Dean. He imagined himself in the school colors, performing on-field for whatever assignment was given to him. College football – the thought of it made his heart race and palms sweat. How many Freshmen had ever even talked with a college coach? Would others come to watch him play? Excitement built within him as he contemplated telling his parents, Lee, Michael, and especially Luke and Timmy, about this ample opportunity. He returned to reality when Coach Dean's voice cut through his reverie, "Any questions for him?"

"Uh, no, I don't. It sounds like a great program. Thank you so much for talking with me." Damian said with a smile, not having heard a single thing Coach Willis had said.

"Not a problem, glad to hear that!" Coach Willis said with a smile. He pulled a sheet of paper out of his bag and handed it to Damian. "This is for you. We have some dates where we're inviting a few prospects to tour the campus and a summer camp we run. It's only an orientation, but it'll give you an idea of what the school offers and meet the coaches. Here's my card, call me when you know what day works for you and your parents." He pulled a business card out of his wallet and handed it to Damian. "On the back, we are also hosting a camp this year. You'd stay in one of the dorms with another player, work out with us during the day, and hang out with staff and current players at night. Talk it over with your parents. If they give a thumbs-up, there's a link to sign up."

Damian searched for the words to thank Coach Willis, failing for a moment before saying, "I will coach; this is awesome. Thank you." He couldn't stop smiling.

He smiled back and shook hands with both Damian and Coach Dean. "We'll be in touch." Coach Willis said as he ducted below the door frame and left the room.

Damian sunk back into the chair, his face beaming with enthusiasm. As he made plans to tell his parents and pick a date to visit, his arm shot up in celebration - only to stop abruptly as he remembered that Coach Dean was still in the room. A wave of embarrassment flushed through him.

"Glad to see you all excited," Coach Dean said, "But before you go, I have a question for you." Confused, Damian nodded to show he was listening. "What's going on with Jared?" Damian shrugged his shoulders, not knowing what to say. "I'm asking because all I hear these days is how he's missing class or not doing the work. Now, you know we're working with low numbers here. Please talk with him and tell him to get it together. Could you do that for me?"

Damian's body tensed, and his mouth went dry. Why was it his responsibility to fix Jared? Then, he couldn't help but think of next season and how they'd need him. He slowly exhaled, then spoke in a quiet voice. "I'll talk to him, but he's got to take care of himself. I can try to help, but ultimately, it's up to him."

"I know. I appreciate any help you can give. And congrats, I'm glad you like Coach Willis and Gettysburg. It's a small school, but it'll be good for you to see the campus too. You

Frost boys are something else!"

Any unsureness quickly vanished with that compliment—the Frost Boys. Damian liked the sounds of that, even if he didn't know what to say to Jared.

As he walked out of the office, his confidence was boosted, and his heartbeat was filled with anticipation. While driving home, he pondered what to tell Jared to put him on the right path again. It wouldn't be a simple task, but he understood it was something he accepted to attempt.

When he arrived home, Damian went straight to his room and took his phone out to call Jared. When he answered, he could tell he was sprawled on the bed, lazily playing video games. "Hey man, what up?" Jared asked.

Taking a deep breath, Damian steeled himself and asked, "Hey, where have you been? I haven't heard or seen you around in a while."

Jared sounded annoyed, "Don't worry about it. I'm doing my own thing. I'm fine. I don't need a babysitter, Mr. Football Star."

Damian felt a twinge of irritation, but he pushed it aside. "That's not what I'm talking about. Coach Dean has noticed that you've missed class and not done your work. He asked me to talk to you and see if I can help."

Jared let out a bitter laugh. "Of course, he did. He's always on my case. Look, I'm fine. I don't feel like doing anything right now, you know? It's the end of the year."

Damian sighed. "I get it. But you can't keep slacking off like this. We need you next year, you know? Seriously. And more than that, you need to take care of yourself. If you keep this up..."

Jared was quiet for a moment. "Yeah, I know."

Damian could sense that Jared was more receptive now. "So, what's going on? Is there anything I can do to help?"

Jared hesitated before opening. "Honestly, it's been hard to get motivated to do anything lately."

Damian listened attentively, trying to understand where Jared was coming from. "Is there something specific that's been bothering you?"

Jared let out a deep sigh. "It's everything, man. School, family stuff, Theresa drama. It feels like everything's piling up, and I can't handle it all."

Damian nodded understandingly. "I get it. But you can't let that bring you down. You're stronger than that. And if you need help, you know I'm here for you. We all are."

Jared was quiet for a moment before responding. "Thanks, man. I appreciate it. Maybe we can study together sometime? I won't ditch you like last time, haha."

Damian smiled, once again holding back his irritation. "Of course. That's what teammates are for, right?"

Jared chuckled. "Yeah, I guess so. Thanks again, Damian."

"No problem, man. Take care of yourself."

As Damian hung up the phone, he felt a sense of relief wash over him. He knew that talking to Jared wouldn't magically solve everything, but it was a start. He was determined to be there for his friend and help him through whatever he was going through. After all, that's what being a teammate was all about.

With his phone safely stowed away, Damian's mind wandered to the possibility of Gettysburg. He was eager and anxious to explore the school and make an informed decision about his future. He recognized that this wasn't going to be a simple choice, but he was elated for the opportunity to pursue his aspirations.

Damian inhaled deeply and laid back in bed, anticipating the future mounting. His eyelids fluttered shut as he waited to discover what would come.

CHAPTER 17 - MR. FROST

"Greetings," Damian tapped on the keyboard, "I hope you've been doing well since our last conversation. It's been a week since the school year finished, and I wanted to check in about any job openings your district may have. I've been subbing for a few months and keeping up with the county website for postings. You said new teacher positions would be available for the upcoming term, but nothing has been posted yet. As of today, July 13th, I'd like to throw my hat in the running for consideration if that is an option. If need be, I'm also available to help in any way I can. Have an excellent day. Best regards, Damian Frost."

His finger hovered over the "enter" key as he read through his email one last time, checking for spelling errors. Satisfied that the message was flawless, he clicked send and watched the screen turn blue with confirmation. He leaned back against the plush fabric of his parent's living room couch, relieved, allowing himself a deep breath before pushing himself up to stand.

Damian sat in front of his computer with bated breath, hoping to see a posting that would allow him to start teaching again. His fingers tapped against the keyboard in frustration, and he watched the page impatiently as it refreshed several times a day. He'd been waiting weeks for a job advertisement for an English teacher position, but while there were plenty of vacancies for science and history teachers, none seemed open in his field. As August crept closer on the calendar, Damian's anxiety rose. He knew soon enough, these positions would be filled; he hoped he would be chosen too.

The summer days seemed to stretch on endlessly—with the schools out and no job, he had nothing to do. Damian would stay up late watching YouTube videos till the morning light, hoping that something in his life would change. Then, one day, a seasonal position opened at a local sandwich shop, and he took it without hesitation. His father's maxim, "Time is Money," had become his mantra.

A week passed, and Damian felt disappointed that he had not heard back from his old teacher. He could barely concentrate on wrapping up the sandwich order for a customer when the chimes of the store door opening stirred him from his thoughts. Looking up, Damian saw Michael standing tall and beaming broadly with Barrett. The color drained from Damian's face as he sheepishly waved back at his former student, feeling embarrassed to see him out of the classroom setting.

"Hey man, I didn't know you were working here?" Michael said as the two friends shook hands.

"Yeah, it's temporary. No work during the Summer. You know what I mean."

"Nah, I get it, man," Michael said as he slapped Barrett's back loudly. Barrett grimiest in pain, then seemingly laughed it off. "Go on, tell him the good news."

"What news?" Damian asked.

Barrett shifted his weight from one foot to the other, eyes glued to the ground. Damian watched him in silence, feeling a familiar discomfort that made its way into his stomach. The air was heavy and thick with unspoken words. Finally, Barrett broke the tension by clearing his throat and speaking.

"I wanted to say thank you for your help earlier this school year. You were right about what mattered most." His voice wavered, but he held Damian's gaze. "I put class before sports, and I'm thankful for it. I've been visiting college campuses, and I'm walking on at Tech next fall. Coach says if I maintain my grades, I might have a scholarship opportunity next year."

"That's awesome. Better late than never, right." Damian said as he reached out his fist to bump. Barrett smiled and did the same. "Glad to see that everything worked out."

"Yeah, we're all excited for him in the family too. So, have you heard about a full-time position yet?" Michael asked.

"No, nothing yet. Looking a little bleak, to be honest, on that front." Damian's smile quickly faded. "Might end up substituting another year now."

"That sucks. I'm sorry. But what about your sister-in-law's suggestion? Government contracting and all? They must be hiring all year round. Plus, I'm sure the money is good."

"Yeah," Damian said unenthusiastically, "I don't know. The money would be much better than substituting, but I'd be stuck at a desk all day. I'm not sure if I want that."

"I get that, but you know, when opportunity knocks. Might be worth looking into."

Damian pushed his hands into the pockets of his faded jeans and stared out the window as he processed Michael's words. It was an excellent chance to get off his feet and move from manual labor to something more administrative, but teaching had long been Damian's passion. He could take this job at the desk for now and keep an eye out for open positions for when next year rolls around.

"Have you heard from Jared lately?" Michael said, jogging Damian out of his thoughts.

"No, not since winter break. Why?"

"He's at his mom's now, came up for her birthday this week. Visit him before he leaves. He's always talking about you and telling stories from when we were kids. He's headed back down to Richmond soon."

"Yeah, I will. It'll be good to see him."

Michael gave a single, decisive nod as Barrett reached out his hand. Their palms met, and the corners of their mouths turned up in relief. The two stood momentarily before Michael opened the door and walked out into the afternoon sun.

Damian drove slowly past Jared's old house, taking in the familiar sights of the weathered wooden plank fence, the patchy lawn, and the cracked concrete walkway. As he got closer to the house, he noticed someone sitting on the porch— it was Jared, the same person who had been there all those years ago. Smoke wafted from a cigarette between his fingers.

As Damian stepped out of his car, the smooth sounds of a saxophone drifted towards him on the breeze. The melody was like a warm hug, wrapping around him and easing the tension in his shoulders. He closed his eyes and momentarily let himself get lost in the music, imagining he was in some swanky speakeasy instead of a dingy neighborhood street. Eventually, he opened his eyes and headed toward the source of the enchanting tunes, feeling lighter than before.

"Jared!" Damian yelled out as he approached the porch. Jared's eyes lit up as he realized that Damian was coming. He greeted his friend and smiled, "How the hell are you, Damian? Go on, grab a seat."

"I'm doing well, man; how are you?" Damian said as he sat and tried to ignore the smell of marijuana around him. "How's Richmond?"

"It's good, it's good. There's not much to say, to be honest. Just working and chilling. You know how it is."

"Michael said you were up here to see your mom; she was around. It's been years, how's she doing? She probably wouldn't recognize me anymore." The smell of marijuana was ever present on the porch, which wasn't much different than when they were kids. Jared didn't look much different, wearing an old Crossroads High School ball cap.

"You just missed her, but she's doing well. Being Miss Independent and all these days." Jared laughed, "How are your folks?" The smell was becoming more potent the longer Damian remained in conversation.

"Oh well, you know. Same old, same old. They never change." Damian chuckled softly as he sat in a chair across from Jared. "You're still smoking weed again, huh." He tried to say jokingly, even though his intention was known.

"Man, don't start with all that. I will do what I want. It settles me."

Damian raised his hands in a sign of surrender, knowing that any further attempts to dissuade him from smoking marijuana would be met with anger. He clamped his lips shut and looked away, not wanting an argument.

"So, how long are you here till?"

"Not sure. I'm considering moving back here once I get my money right." The irony passed Damian's mind as he watched Jared flick the ashes from his joint before resting it on the table. "The drive back and forth to see my mom is a lot, and I don't know. Cash is always tight, it seems." He picked up the joint once again and inhaled deeply. "I'm lonely down there without you all too. Not the same as it used to be. It's too much alone time, know what I mean?"

"I guess that makes sense. Is your mom ok with that? I remember her talking about throwing a party when you moved out." Damian responded jokingly.

"Man, whatever," Jared laughed, "She misses me, I know it!"

It wasn't a joke that Damian had made. At their high school graduation party, Damian remembered watching with trepidation as Jared's mother stumbled around with a glass of red wine. Her laughter rang throughout the room. She joyfully proclaimed that she was free now that he was off to college or away from her home.

"What are you going to do for work?" Damian asked. "When you move back, I mean."

"No idea, I guess I'll figure it out." Jared said as he shifted around in his chair and set down the joint, "Did you ever get a full-time teaching job?"

"No, still no word." Damian sighed and shook his head, defeated. "Sucks."

"So, what are you going to do for work then?" Jared asked in a slightly mocking tone.

Damian, flabbergasted, chuckled to himself, then looked up at his friend and said, "No idea, I guess I'll figure it out as well."

Damian and Jared shared a smile, both knowing their respective plights. Damian's gaze softened as he thought of his friend's hard luck. He was blessed to have a family and the means to support himself, even if he wasn't thrilled with living at home. Damian had options, even if this teaching job didn't work out. The two men shared a mutual understanding, commiserating in their different circumstances and offering each other silent support.

Damian's eyes darted to his watch as he stood on the wooden bench and brushed off his jeans. He let out a sigh, then turned to his friend. "I guess it's time for me to hit the dusty trail," he said, holding his hand.

They shook hands firmly, and Damian beamed at his friend. "Let me know when you're coming back up," he said with a smile. "We'll grab some water."

As he walked away, Damian took one last look over his shoulder at Jared, sitting contently on the front stoop of his mother's home. Something about Jared's demeanor only made Damian more curious about him. A sense of intrigue and mystery had always surrounded his friend, and Damian couldn't shake the feeling that he was not being entirely truthful about his life.

"Bet," Jared said, smiling in return.

"Take care of yourself, man. Take it seriously," Damian said as he walked toward his car and drove down the road.

Pulling into the driveway, Damian pondered his odds of getting a teaching job for the upcoming school year. He'd likely need to wait two or three weeks for background checks and onboarding, meaning it would be well into August before he could start working. That gave everyone else a two-week advantage on him. It wasn't likely that any positions would even be offered by then.

Damian stood in the middle of his room, contemplating. He had debated for months whether to take Gretchen up on her offer and now he knew what he wanted to do. His fingers trembled slightly as he unlocked his phone and sent a text asking for an application link. Seconds later, his phone buzzed with an excited reply from Gretchen, wishing him luck. He hadn't felt so hopeful in weeks.

When Damian read the text message on his phone, he thought, "Maybe this is my lucky moment. " He then put his phone on hold, anticipating what was to come.

CHAPTER 18 - DAMIAN

amian's pencil drummed impatiently on his desk as he stared out the window, daydreaming of a time when he wasn't consumed by school work. The classroom was oppressively still, except for the rhythmic ticking of the clock. He half-heartedly scribbled answers onto the worksheet before him, glancing up every few minutes to check how much time was left until the bell rang. With no sports or tests to occupy his mind, each school day felt agonizingly slow and endless.

With his English worksheet completed, he strolled to the front of the class and handed it to Ms. Grey. As she scanned the answers with a furrowed brow, he couldn't help but glance out the window at the track and field coaches marking outlines for that afternoon's practice. He should have joined and thrown the shotput instead of spending his afternoons feeling bored at home. He made a mental note to join the team for something to do after school next year.

As Ms. Grey finished reviewing Damian's English worksheet, she looked up at him with a small smile playing on her lips. "Well done, Damian," she said, her voice warm and encouraging. I'm not surprised; you've done great all year long." She handed the sheet back to Damian.

"Thank you, Ms. Grey," Damian replied with a sheepish smile, his cheeks flushing slightly at the unexpected praise.

As the bell rang and his classmates swiftly gathered their belongings to head out for lunch, Ms. Grey softly called out to Damian, "Damian, could you please stay behind for a moment? I'd like to have a word with you."

Curiosity piqued, Damian watched as his friends filed out of the classroom, leaving him alone with his English teacher. Ms. Grey walked over to her desk and motioned for Damian to sit in front of her. The sunlight streaming through the window cast a warm glow around them.

"I've been meaning to talk to you about your writing," Ms. Grey began, her voice gentle yet earnest. "There's a…" A knock at the classroom door interrupted her, as the two of them turned to see who it was.

"Am I too late?" Mr. Anderson said, peering around the corner of the door.

"Not at all. I was just starting. Please come in, " she said with a grin. Damian watched in confusion as two of his teachers sat in front of him.

Ms. Grey began again once Mr. Anderson took his seat. "I've told Mr. Anderson how well your writing has improved this year." Damian felt a blush coming on and did his best to hide it.

"There's depth to it, and honesty in your words is captivating," Mr. Anderson added, his gaze intently on Damian. "Have you ever considered joining the school newspaper, Damian? We think you have a real talent for storytelling and reporting."

The idea of joining the school newspaper had never crossed his mind before. Writing had always been a private passion, and it was to make sense of the world around him. To share his thoughts and stories with a broader audience seemed daunting yet thrilling.

"I… I've never really thought about it," Damian admitted, feeling a surge of self-doubt at the idea of putting himself out there in such a public way. "I mean, I enjoy writing, but I'm not sure others would enjoy reading what I write."

Ms. Grey smiled reassuringly at Damian. "Your writing has a unique voice and perspective that we believe would make a valuable contribution to our school paper. I'm sure others in school would agree."

Mr. Anderson nodded in agreement. "Don't underestimate the impact your words can have on those around you. We both think you'd do well."

Damian sat there, stunned by his teachers' unexpected praise and encouragement. The idea of joining the school newspaper began to take root in his mind, filling him with excitement and nervousness.

After a moment of contemplative silence, Damian looked up at Ms. Grey and Mr. Anderson with newfound determination in his eyes. "I'll do it," he said quietly but firmly. "I'll join the school newspaper."

A bright smile spread across Ms. Grey's face, her eyes sparkling with pride. "That's wonderful to hear, Damian. I can't wait to see what stories you'll bring to life with your writing."

Mr. Anderson clapped Damian on the shoulder, a supportive gesture that filled Damian with a sense of belonging and purpose.

As Damian left the classroom, his mind was already brimming with ideas for his first story. He wanted it to be something he was interested in and something that others might be interested in. Then it hit him - Michael's next baseball game.

With his athletic frame and focused gaze, Michael was the undeniable star player of their school's baseball team even as a freshman. He was a natural talent on the field with a big arm that could precisely throw strikes. His powerful swings and swift base-running always captivate the crowds. Writing about him and the team's upcoming game would perfectly showcase his storytelling abilities.

Damian attended the game later that day, and then that evening, Damian sat down at his desk, a blank page staring back at him. With a deep breath, he began to weave a story of determination and triumph on the baseball diamond. He described the crisp spring air, the crowd's roar, and the game's intensity as Michael stepped up to bat.

As Damian poured his heart and soul into his writing, he lost track of time, completely immersed in the world he created. He detailed Michael's focused expression as he eyed the pitcher, the tension in the air palpable as the game hung in the balance. With each swing of the bat, Damian painted a vivid picture of the crack of the ball against the wooden bat, sending it soaring into the distance.

Amidst the crowd's roaring, cheerleaders' feet pounded against the dirt as he sprinted around the bases. His cleats dug into the ground, sending up plumes of dust in his wake, adding to the frantic energy of the game. Damian's words flowed effortlessly onto the page, capturing every detail and emotion of the moment - the pounding heartbeats, the adrenaline rush, and the electric excitement that pulsed through the stands. It was as if the readers were transported to the edge of their seats, experiencing every exhilarating moment alongside Michael and his team.

As Michael slid into home plate, a triumphant smile on his face, Damian felt a surge of pride at having translated this moment of victory into a tale that shimmered with life. He knew this story would resonate with his peers, drawing them into the thrill of the game and celebrating Michael's talent on the field.

When Damian finally placed his pen down, he knew he had created something special. Students eagerly flipped through the school newspaper when the following paper was released. Damian's story about Michael's baseball game was met with an overwhelmingly positive response. The vivid descriptions and emotional depth with which he captured the essence of the game had readers on the edge of their seats, feeling as if they were part of the action themselves.

Michael himself read the article with pride and gratitude, touched by Damian's ability to encapsulate the game's intensity and his passion for playing. He sought out Damian in the bustling hallways, smiling as he clasped his friend's shoulder in appreciation.

"Man, you captured the spirit of that game," Michael said, his eyes shining with admiration. "I felt like I was reliving every moment through your words. Thank you for sharing it with everyone."

Damian beamed at Michael's words, feeling a swell of happiness and validation in his chest. The positive feedback from his peers and the subject of his story meant more to him than he could express.

Encouraged by the success of his first article, Damian dove headfirst into his role at the school newspaper, seeking out new stories to tell and experiences to capture in his writing.

He covered everything from student achievements to local events, infusing each piece with his unique perspective and storytelling prowess.

Damian's reputation as a talented writer grew throughout the school with each article he published, earning him praise and admiration from classmates and teachers alike. His pieces became eagerly anticipated reads, with students discussing and dissecting his latest works in the halls between classes.

As Damian sat in the school library, working on his final story of the school year, he suddenly felt a presence beside him. Looking up, he saw a familiar face peering down at his work with keen interest. It was Ms. Grey, her eyes alight with pride and admiration.

"Damian, I wanted to tell you how impressed I am with your writing growth," she said warmly. "Your storytelling has evolved in ways I could have only imagined when we first spoke about joining the school newspaper."

"Thank you, Ms. Grey," Damian replied, a warmth spreading at her words. He respected and admired Ms. Grey as a teacher and someone who had nurtured his passion for writing and believed in his potential.

Ms. Grey cleared her throat, adjusting her glasses with a small smile playing on her lips. "I have some exciting news to share with you, Damian. Next year, we will introduce a new elective class called journalism, and I truly believe it would be a perfect fit for someone with your talent and passion for storytelling."

Damian's eyes widened in excitement at the prospect of delving even deeper into the world of journalism, of having the opportunity to further hone his skills and explore his writing more.

"I think you would excel in the course, Damian," Ms. Grey continued. "It will allow you to continue writing captivating stories and learn about different forms of journalism, from investigative reporting to feature articles."

A surge of determination welled within Damian as he listened to Ms. Grey's words of encouragement. The thought of expanding his writing horizons and delving into the world of journalism ignited something within him.

"I would love to be a part of the journalism class, Ms. Grey," Damian said, his voice overflowing with anticipation. "It sounds like an incredible opportunity."

Ms. Grey beamed with pride, her belief in Damian's potential shining brightly in her eyes. "I knew you would be excited about this, Damian. Your eagerness for writing is truly inspiring, and I do not doubt you will make a remarkable journalist someday."

As summer approached, Damian's excitement grew with each passing day. Not only would he finally be free from his grueling freshman year of high school, but the possibilities for his future seemed endless.

CHAPTER 19 - MR. FROST

Damian gazed at the towering structure from his spot on the street corner. The windows, lined with mirrors, shone brilliantly in the early morning light, casting reflections on the surrounding trees and passing vehicles.

He stood there fidgeting in his ill-fitting suit. It was a few sizes too small for him to feel comfortable, but he couldn't complain - his mother had found it marked down at a discount store and insisted it would make a great first impression on his new boss if he wore it.

Today was his first day as an Administrative Assistant with the Department of Justice contracting office, where they handled funding for government vendors. He wasn't sure what that meant exactly, but he saw it as an opportunity to earn some money until something better came along. Beggars can't be choosers, after all.

His tie felt too tight, but he couldn't fix it now. Not standing on the street corner surrounded by other well-dressed individuals, all seemingly headed in the same direction as him. He felt out of place surrounded by these people, like an imposter waiting to be ousted.

After entering the building and struggling to navigate

security, he met his new boss, Lauren Glasgow, near the elevators. They had met several times beforehand, once during his second phase interview and once more when he first came to the building to claim his ID badge. She was an average-looking woman with dark hair and an easygoing attitude.

They shook hands, and she pointed towards the elevators to direct them to their 11th-floor office. Eleven floors seemed very high up to Damian, but looking at the buttons on the elevator, he realized it was only halfway up in this building. He couldn't imagine how many people worked here.

"Here's where you'll sit," Lauren said as they arrived at a cubical outside the office entrance. "I'll be right there if you need me. Why don't you settle in and log on to your computer? When you start it up, there are always kinks to work out." Damian smiled awkwardly while setting his bag down. "What's in your bag?"

"Oh, just some supplies. Pens, scissors, that kind of stuff."

"Oh, okay. Well, so you know, you can decorate this cube however you'd like. Within reason of course. Try not to put anything up that disrupts anyone or is inappropriate for work. And, so you know, we have an office closet around the corner if you need anything else." Damian nodded, gesturing a thank you. "I'll send over Gabi in a few minutes to give you your first task. Again, if you need anything, I'm right over there." Lauren said, smiling.

"Thank you so much," Damian said as Lauren acknowledged it and walked to her office.

The cubicle itself was spacious but the very definition of sterile. It had a light gray plastic table with equally gray lockers at the entrance. There were also cabinets in the cubicle above more desk, which were also several shades of gray, but this time with a streak of blue to break up the monotony.

A keyboard and two mounted monitors connected to a docking station were on one of the two desks. Damian could mount his computer and use the two screens. High tech, to say the least, as he only used a small laptop as a substitute at best. The other desk was almost barren except for a large black cube in the middle. It looked like a small printer with no tray to hold the paper. It must have held some use, but for now, Damian ignored it while taking his first seat in his desk chair.

After setting up his profile, Damian sat at his desk. He watched as the minutes ticked away on his computer. He tried scrolling through the digital documents he was given to pass the time and update his government profile, but soon, even that didn't help. He felt bored, which is precisely what his sister-in-law said would happen.

Gretchen said, "Your first week will probably be a drag. As you get more tasks, the days will go by faster and faster." She certainly was not wrong about that. Before he knew it, it was 11:30 am, and he still had not heard from anyone named Gabi.

He peaked around his cubicle several times at Lauren's office to see if she was available, but each time he looked, her door was shut, or she was nowhere to be found. She was swamped.

Resolved to wait for his first task, he leaned back in his chair and looked up at the ceiling tiles above him. They were as sterile as the rest of the building and, as uniform, placed next to bright fluorescent lights. He closed his eyes and thought about what might be going on with his students. They must have started classes not too long ago, and he wondered how they were acting with a new school year ahead of them. He asked if Barrett was still doing well and if Mr. Kraft was still laughing loudly at poorly told jokes from his students.

As he sat there thinking, a knock on his locker quickly brought him back to reality, and he jerked sharply to see who it was. A woman stood at the entrance of his cubicle. She was plump, with a curly head of hair and a sly grin on her face. "Didn't wake you, did I?" she said jokingly.

"No, no. Just daydreaming is all. You must be Gabi?"

"Must I?" She responded. Confused, Damian nodded, seemingly relaying he didn't know who else she'd be. "Well, you're correct. My name is Gabi, and I'm told you need something to do, right?"

"Right," Damian replied.

"Follow me," She waved her hand towards her and started walking down the corridor where the other cubicles lay. They walked together relatively quickly, and Damian did his best to stay in lockstep with her. "Got to move fast around here. Slow work means no work." Gabi said as she charged ahead.

She stopped suddenly at the door marked File Room 1134B. She turned to Damian and said, "Here's where you'll be working today. We have some files that need to be sorted, and I think you're the man for the job." Gabi smiled and opened the door, motioning for Damian to follow her inside.

The file room was chilly, lit by a dim fluorescent bulb that hung from the ceiling. The walls were lined with metal filing cabinets, and stacks of paper were piled high on the ground. The room smelled of dust and old paper, making Damian want to sneeze.

"Okay, so the files we need you to sort are in these boxes," Gabi said, pointing to several cardboard boxes stacked in the corner. "All you have to do is go through them, find the correct file, and put it in the correct folder. Easy peasy, right?"

Damian nodded, "Yeah, I can do that."

"Good," Gabi said, "I'll come back in a few hours to check on your progress. Don't worry, it's not as tedious as it looks. Just think of it as a puzzle that needs to be solved."

Damian watched Gabi leave the file room, closing the door behind her. He was left alone in the chilly, quiet room with only the files and cabinets for company. He took a deep breath and started to work, grabbing the first box of files and sorting them individually.

Damian was lost in thought as he worked, his hands methodically moving from one task to the next. He had left behind a career for which he had been passionate and well-loved, feeling that the stability of this job was worth more than the constant uncertainty of substitute work. But as he worked, his mind filled with images of his students, their enthusiasm, and joy when they learned something new. He felt a deep pang of regret, wondering if he had made the right decision.

Damian's elbows rested on the table, and his forehead wrinkled in frustration. He had been sorting through paperwork for hours, a seemingly never-ending stack of yellowing documents piled high in front of him. The slow ticking of the clock echoed off the walls, and each minute felt like an eternity. As if on cue, Gabi returned to check on Damian's progress, her shoes clicking against the marble floor.

"How's it going in here?" She said with a mocking grin.

Damian placed the folder he was holding down and centered himself. "Well, it's going. I feel like I haven't even made a dent." He chuckled to lighten his mood.

"Don't be surprised if that pile never gets smaller. It's the government, there is lots of paperwork going from one office to another. You'll probably have a new stack by tomorrow morning." Damian's stomach sank, thinking about filing more.

"Anyway, it's lunchtime. Want to come with us? We're heading to this deli around the block."

"Yeah, that sounds great. Thanks," Damian replied.

The three stepped into the shiny elevator and rode it silently down to the lobby. As they emerged into the busy space, Damian reached for his phone, only to realize that he hadn't been able to send or receive any messages while in the filing room. When he touched the screen, dozens of notifications pinged to life—mainly from Michael and some from friends he hadn't seen or heard from since high school. He focused as he scrolled through the names and dates of each missed call and unread message.

As he scrolled, his phone suddenly rang out. It was a call from Michael. Answering it, Damian said, "Hello, Michael? Sorry, I see I missed a ton of calls. My office has a terrible signal. What happened?"

The line was silent, and it seemed to stretch forever. Sudden static muffled Michael's voice before he spoke again with a hint of desperation. "Damian, Jared's gone. They found him in his apartment this morning." Damian felt the air leave his lungs as his heart dropped into his stomach.

He was frozen, not knowing how to express the shock that had filled his body. His mind raced with questions as his lips formed a whispered plea of "Jesus..." hoping for some sign or answer but not expecting one.

Damian's heart raced as he listened to the voice on the other end of the line. "Jared's gone," the person repeated, but their words seemed far away, muffled by the deafening roar in Damian's ears. He gripped the phone so tightly that his hands became numb, trying to make sense of this unimaginable news. His mind whirled with confusion and disbelief, searching for a logical explanation.

"How could Jared be gone? We talked not long ago." Damian thought. He struggled to hold back tears, desperate for any information that could bring him peace or understanding.

A briefcase slapped against the ground in the lobby, jolting him out of his thoughts. He quickly placed his phone in his pocket, and straightened his back before taking a few deep breaths to calm himself. He remained silent the remainder of the day, smiling when necessary and generally keeping his thoughts and feelings to himself. That was until he reached his vehicle to go home, where everything flooded out.

CHAPTER 20 - DAMIAN

"So, I have some news, guys," Michael said while he, Damian and Jared walked home from their morning weight room workout. It was a sunny summer day, perfect for a dip in a pool or a game of basketball at the park.

"I, uh," Michael continued, struggling to find the words. "My dad and I talked with a coach from St. David High School, and they're offering to cover my tuition to play baseball there next year. So, I won't be going to Crossroads next year with y'all."

Damian and Jared kept walking, looking at each other and the ground in front of them, not knowing what to say. Then, like a strike of a match, Damian exclaimed, "You're what?" followed by Jared saying, "Yeah, are you serious?"

Silence overtook the group as everyone awkwardly kept walking while thoughts flew through their minds.

"Look, it's good news. You know I want to play college ball one day, maybe even pro, and St. David has a great program." Michael said, breaking the silence.

"Yeah, no, you're right. That is awesome man. We're going to miss you, that's all. It won't be the same with you missing." Damian said, staying positive, though inside, he was distraught at the news. Michael had been his best friend. They'd spent almost every day with each other for years now. And though he was happy to see his friend succeed, they'd see each other less now, possibly only on weekends.

"Thank you, Damian," Michael said. "And look, I'm still going to be in the neighborhood. Down the street like always, you know?"

"Exactly," Damian affirmed, forcing a grin on his face.

"No," Jared said with a note of frustration. "Not exactly. You're going to hardly see us, bro, not like normal. You're going to be around rich kids and hanging out with them. You'll forget all about us."

"That's not true!" Michael said, reflecting the same tone as Jared. "I'm still the same guy dude. Don't be like that. We're still going to hang out like always."

"Sure," Jared said with contempt.

Jared kept silent for some time after that. Damian could see that the news might have been too much for him to hear. He felt a great deal of pain at the news as well, but he did whatever he could so that Michael wouldn't know it. Damian smiled and was supportive no matter how hard it was to lose a friend by his side each day.

Jared paused his play when he heard his phone ringing. He picked it up, apprehensive as he read the screen on the device. After taking a moment to internalize what he'd seen, Jared uttered ironically, "Great! More good news!" "What is it?" Michael asked as he and Damian looked at each other, confused.

"Theresa's on her way here. She said her sister drove by and saw us up here. God, I don't want to deal with this too."

Trying not to sound eager to see her, Damian stepped up and said, "Really? I haven't seen her in a while. I mean, it is up to you, man. If it's uncomfortable for you, we get it." Damian paused, breathing, afraid that he might have offended Jared.

Thankfully, Michael encouraged her to join them: "We all haven't hung out in some time, man. It might be nice."

Jared looked at the two of them, annoyed and unsure if he wanted to see her. But, succumbing to the pressure, he accepted it and texted her back, letting her know that they'd wait for her.

Damian, again trying not to seem happy at this outcome, began dribbling the basketball and shooting it at the hoop. Inside, though, he was elated. They had only seen each other in passing, sometimes in the halls, sometimes after school, each time they were with other friends or in a hurry off somewhere. And even if they had met, it was awkward. Had Jared seen them together, he'd have gotten upset, plus Damian didn't know how not to ask what happened between them. Avoiding each other seemed easier than addressing that.

Now, though, sometime between their breakup might be a perfect time to reconnect. With Michael going to another school, he'd need another friend to fill those shoes.

When Theresa arrived, Michael and Damian were the first to greet her. They hugged and welcomed her as old friends do. Jared quietly stepped forward and waved, saying, "Hey, Theresa." faintly.

"Hey, Jared," Theresa said in an equally low tone.

Damian held his breath, feeling the tension between them and hoping for the best. He wasn't sure if either could handle hanging out again like they had in the past.

Then, thankfully, Jared smiled at Theresa and said, "How have you been?"

"Good, I've been good. You?" She responded.

"I've been good too," Jared said as Damian exhaled in relief.

Damian was happy to see the whole gang back together. It had been a weird year with Jared and Theresa's situation and adjusting to the high school life in general. But now things seemed normal, at least as much as possible. Michael would not be with them in a few months, and Damian still had some irritations with Jared, but when they were all together in the same space, he knew they'd be just fine.

Later that night, while Damian sat on the couch watching TV with his father, he began to wonder if this was how things would be from now on. He knew that every year would bring new situations that would stress his relationships with his friends, and shape his views on them. He thought about how the next football season might go and if he would be able to keep Jared eligible to play, as he suspected Coach Dean would once again ask him to help. Would he and Theresa ever be as close as they were before?

"You okay, son?" Damian's father asked. Damian turned to look at him, realizing he was making a face while thinking.

"Yeah, I'm fine… Well, can I ask you a question?" Damian asked.

"Sure, I might even have an answer for you."

"Why do things have to change so much? Michaels will be going to that private school I told you about, and I don't know, I feel like how I am around Jared is different than it used to be. It's only been a year, and things are different. Is that normal?

"His father thought for a minute, obviously trying to gather his thoughts, and then said, "You know, I wish I could say that things will always be good or how they should be with your friends or anyone in your life. But things change, Damian, not always for the better or the worse. That's life. But, if you stay true to yourself and do what you think or feel is best, I can say things generally work themselves out. Not always how you expect it."

Damian sat with his words momentarily, thinking about them and coming to terms with how his life might go. He looked at his dad and smirked, nodding to him in agreement.

His father smiled back and said, "My grandfather used to say that life was not a straight, paved road. Instead, it's an old, beat up gravel road, full of odd-shaped rocks, dips and pits, and rugged hills. And you're driving a sedan." His dad chuckled, and Damian couldn't help but join him. "The important thing to remember is that everyone has their road to travel, full of the same issues you'll encounter. Have faith that they'll figure it out as you will."

Free of thought, Damian looked at his father, smiled, and said, "Thanks, Dad."

Damian thought often of his conversation with his father as the days turned into weeks. He played it repeatedly in his head, finding comfort in the words that urged him to embrace change and trust in the path ahead.

With Michael's impending departure to a private school, Damian knew their friendship would be tested. They promised to keep in touch and do their best to spend time together during breaks, but Damian couldn't shake the feeling of loss deep down. It was like a part of his daily routine was slowly slipping away.

But Damian was determined to make the most of their remaining time together. Every day that summer, he and Michael would meet at their favorite spot in the park, playing basketball until the sun set behind the trees, or they'd meet at each other's home, playing video games all hours of the night. They laughed and talked, cherishing each moment as if it were their last.

Meanwhile, Jared and Theresa seemed to have rekindled their friendship, and Damian watched them from a distance, happy to see his friends finding solace in each other's company once again. He would need them both, with Michael going his own way now.

One day in late July, as Damian sat in his room, lost in his thoughts and bored, he looked over at a stack of books left in his room by his mother. Earlier that week, she started throwing things away in the house, a summer cleaning. She found some old books they'd collected over the years and left them for Damian to go through in case he wanted them.

He stood up, walked towards the stack, and looked through them to see if anything piqued his interest. There was a history book of the NFL, which he'd looked through multiple times as a kid to see the pictures of former players, a collection of Hardy Boys books, and a few other books that didn't seem all that interesting to Damian.

Then, he found an old paperback edition of Mary Shelley's Frankenstein at the bottom of the stack. It was taped up to keep the binding together and had a stamp on the inside cover that read "Property of the Crossroads High School Library." Lee likely took this book out for reading in a class one day and never returned it. Its pages were well read, bent in many corners and turning brown.

Damian examined the book for a moment, debating whether he should read it or not. He had heard of Frankenstein before, the iconic tale of a mad scientist and the monster he creates, but he wasn't sure if it would be his cup of tea. Something about the worn-out pages intrigued him though as he took the book with him.

Settling back onto his bed, Damian opened the book and began to read. From the first page, he was drawn into the story of Dr. Victor Frankenstein and his creation. It was nothing like he'd seen in the movies. It was poetic, a dance of colorful language and imagery that danced in his mind as he read each word. The themes of loneliness, ambition resonated with him more profoundly than expected.

With each passing chapter, Damian found himself questioning his actions and motives. Had he been a good friend to Michael, supporting his decision to attend the private school? Or had he allowed jealousy and fear of losing their friendship to cloud his judgment? And with Jared and Theresa, had he truly forgiven them for their past mistakes, or was there still a lingering resentment that prevented their bond from fully healing?

As the sun went down, Damian turned the novel's last page. It dawned on him that he'd never read a book all the way through before, not like this at least. In class, they'd read, but most of the time, there was a movie they'd watch after or a recording they'd listen to. Because of this, Damian would only pay half attention, waiting for the movie to retell the necessary parts for him.

He liked this feeling, this introspection brought on by reading. It felt therapeutic in a way. It was a time to relax and take in what the book was saying, away from whatever was happening in his life. It was an escape from everything. He placed the book on his bedside table and again looked at the stack of books. He grabbed the next novel in the stack and continued his escape.

CHAPTER 21 - MR. FROST

Damian pulled into the cemetery's parking lot, his headlights briefly illuminating the grey stone building before he switched them off. He took a deep breath, trying to steel himself against the melancholy atmosphere, before forcing himself out of the car. He had driven past this chapel countless times over the years but never stepped foot inside—not until now.

Damian stood outside the cemetery, admiring the meticulously groomed flower garden and tall monuments in remembrance of those who had passed. He tried to remember Jared's voice, thinking about something his father once told him: "It's not the best part of life, but it is part of it." As he thought about it all, details about Jared's passing remained scanty, leaving room for much speculation. All that was certain was that Jared hadn't answered a call for some time, causing enough worry that his mother decided to check in on him. That's when she found him in his living room. Some thought it was a heart attack, while others suspected that he had relapsed. But nothing was certain, or at this point imperative for that matter.

The chapel was small and dimly lit, but the pews were filled with people. Damian recognized many of them – Jared's family members, high school friends, and even a few former teachers who had attended even though it was a weekday morning. He sat at the back of the room and listened as the pastor shared stories of Jared's life. Occasionally, someone in the crowd would let out a chuckle or quiet sob, demonstrating the range of emotions set afloat by memories of their beloved friend.

As he looked around the crowded funeral service, his eyes landed on many familiar faces from high school. They had all aged, but he could still recognize each one. However, a thin and frail old man seated in the corner of the chapel caught Damian's attention the most. The man's face was notched with anger and sadness as he clutched onto a cane for support. It was clear that he was deeply affected by the loss of life.

Then suddenly, Damian knew precisely who it was. It was Mr. Fritz, their former math teacher, now years older but still exuding an imposing aura. Damian couldn't help but remember Jared's outburst in class, which led to Mr. Fritz leaving his teaching job. He wondered why the seemingly emotionless man had bothered to attend at all. Was it because of some unspoken connection he felt to his former students?

The eulogy began, and Damian's heart became heavy. He could still feel the warmth of their last embrace and recalled how they spent summer days playing catch in the park and lingering late into the night in Damian's basement playing video games. But time had flown by too quickly; now, a wooden coffin at the front of the room was all that remained of his friend.

He remembered how even mentioning Jared's dad had filled him with fear and how his mom had tried to toughen him up in her own way. He wondered if it was too much for him to grow up like that. Did that make him reliant on his friends to hold him up? Did he need his friends to stand shoulder-to-shoulder with him during the dark days when he was so alone? Tears filled his eyes as he realized he had failed him.

His heart felt like it was being crushed beneath a weight of sadness and grief. He stood, head bowed, in the solemn church with the rest of the congregation, quietly reciting prayers for the deceased.

As the eulogy ended, a soft sob escaped from Damian's lips, betraying the facade of composure he had tried so hard to maintain. He felt a hand gently squeeze his shoulder, offering silent, sorrowful solidarity.

Damian composed himself and turned to see whose hand had provided the comfort. He saw Mr. Fritz at his side. His gaze lingered on Damian for a moment before he slowly rose from his seat, his aged frame trembling slightly. Damian was surprised at how quickly and silently the old man made his way over to him.

For a moment, the two sat in silence, looking at one another, and then Mr. Fritz spoke in a surprisingly soft voice, "I remember you, Damian Frost. I remember both you and Jared." His eyes held a deep emotion that Damian had never seen before in the stern teacher's gaze. "I know the weight of grief you carry, the burden of loss that sits heavy on your shoulders."

Damian looked up at Mr. Fritz, his eyes no longer the icy cold blue he remembered as a kid. There was a raw vulnerability in that moment, a shared understanding that transcended the years that had passed since they had been in the classroom together. "You remember us?" Damian whispered, his voice rough with emotion.

Mr. Fritz nodded slowly, his weathered features etched with sadness. "I don't recall much these days. But I remember you and him. You all were my last batch of kids, not my worst." He paused as if grappling with his memories. "I hope things are going well for you, young man, all things considered."

Silence settled between them. Damian searched for the right words to express his conflicting feelings - grief, guilt, and an unexpected sense of irony seeing a teacher he and Jared once shared. Finally, he found his voice hoarse but steady.

"Thank you, Mr. Fritz," Damian began, his words tinged with sincerity. "I… I wish things had turned out differently for Jared. For all of us."

Mr. Fritz's gaze softened, a flicker of understanding passing between them. "Life tends to take us down unexpected paths," he said, his voice gruff yet gentle. "All we can do is hold onto the memories and gain wisdom from the experiences we gain."

"I understand, Mr. Fritz," Damian continued, his voice wavering slightly. "I wish Jared was still here with us. It all feels like a dream, and a cruel one at that." His eyes glistened with unshed tears as he spoke.

Mr. Fritz nodded in quiet agreement, his expression filled with empathy . "Loss is never easy," he said softly. "But Jared will always live on in your memories and in the moments you shared. Hold onto those precious memories, for they will guide you through the darkest times."

With a solemn nod, they both clasped hands, offering each other the best of wishes. "Goodbye, Damian Frost," he said quietly, his voice carrying a weight of years gone by.

Damian and Michael stood in the parking lot, lost in the solemnity of their shared grief. The only sound was the occasional muffled sob. Then, they heard a faint yet unmistakable voice calling them from behind. Damian turned around to find Mr. Anderson walking up with heavy steps. He had also come to pay his last respects.

Damian grabbed Mr. Anderson's hand, his grip firm and reassuring. He waited until Michael copied the gesture before releasing it. "Hey, Mr. Anderson," he said, "How have you been?"

Mr. Anderson's face softened, and his brow creased. He shook his head slowly as he spoke, his voice gentle and sorrowful. "It's just awful," he said. "I had such high hopes for Jared. He was a knucklehead, sure, but there was goodness inside of him. All he needed was some direction. It's heartbreaking what happened." His two friends stood in silence, their faces solemn and eyes downcast.

The trio conversed briefly, with Michael discussing his recent job as a police officer and Damian narrating about his new role.

Mr. Anderson exhaled a long sigh as he looked at his two former students, now men, who had lost their friend in front of him. He placed his hands on their shoulders and tried to give them some sense of comfort. "I understand this day has been hard for both of you," he said gently. "Losing a friend is never easy, especially when they have so much ahead of them. I want to advise you: When fortune knocks at the door, answer it. Don't waste the opportunities that come your way. Life can be over in an instant, and I'd love to hear that you two are making the most of yours." Mr. Anderson stepped back, letting go of their shoulders and giving them one final nod before walking towards his car.

As Mr. Anderson exited, Michael turned to Damian and gave him a firm pat on the back. "Thanks for everything. It means a lot," he said genuinely. They exchanged a warm smile before parting ways.

Damian leaned against the hood of his car with his hands stuffed deep in his pockets as he watched the last few stragglers leave the cemetery. The sky was a deep purple and orange, the sun barely peeking over the horizon. As he pondered his future, a wave of uncertainty washed over him.

No matter his path, he was determined to make it a happy one. He shifted the car into drive and drove off into the sunset, ready to tackle whatever challenges.

As Damian drove away, his sorrow over his friend's passing tugged at his heartstrings. When he arrived home, he was surprised to see his father standing at the door with a cold beer in one hand and an arm outstretched toward him. He was welcomed into a warm, heartfelt embrace before his father said, "I'm so sorry, son. I know you're hurting right now."

"I am," Damian said, "I wish I did more, you know?"

"Unfortunately, I do. I've had a number of my friends pass away as well, most of which could have been saved." Damian's father paused as he looked at his son with sympathy. "But I want you to remember something, Damian. No matter how much good you do, there will always be people who need help, and you can be the one to provide it. It's not your job, but I encourage you to continue trying to help those less fortunate, no matter what life throws at you. You are stronger than you think, and right now, it seems bad, but you will push through it."

As they strolled towards the front door, Damian's father paused to wrap his arm around his son's shoulder. The bright, warm sunlight shone down on them as they walked. "You know," his father said with a smile, "I'm proud of you for always trying to make a difference in someone's life." Damian couldn't help but feel happy at his father's words, and he returned the embrace gratefully. "Even if it doesn't always feel appreciated or remembered," his father continued, "being a good person matters. I'm sure Jared was grateful for everything you did for him."

He gently squeezed Damian's shoulder before they finally entered the house. "It may not always be easy," his father said softly, "but it will always be worth it."

CHAPTER 22 - DAMIAN

August had arrived, and Damian tore open the doors of the school building, his cleats clattering against the tile floors. He wound his way through the halls to his locker, spinning the combination tumblers with a flick of his thumb and forefinger. He grabbed his helmet and shoulder pads, adjusted the straps so they felt snug and secure around him, and exited towards the football field.

The air was cool yet still thick with humidity, promising more heat later in the day. His teammates shuffled past him, some half-asleep, as Damian made his way to the practice area.

His sophomore year on varsity was upon him, a chance for him to truly shine on the team. He was given new gear this season. A lightweight helmet with a softer inner shell, a protective girdle with built-in thigh pads, and sturdy shoulder pads that allowed for more mobility. The gear was much better than he'd received the previous year, just the scraps for the new guys. Damian felt like an absolute warrior in his new equipment and couldn't wait to hit the field.

As Damian approached the field, he could hear Coach Dean's booming voice echoing across the grass. The team was already lined up, sweat glistening on their foreheads as they braced themselves for the first grueling practice of the season. "Let's go, boys!" Coach Dean hollered, his whistle hanging from his neck as he paced back and forth. "This season is ours for the taking! Show me what you've got!"

The team erupted in cheers, and Damian felt a thrill of excitement run through him. Even Jared seemed ready to take on this season despite how early it was this morning. Damian took a deep breath, feeling the weight of his team's expectations and his determination to make this season his most successful.

As the drills began, Damian felt his muscles stretch and flex, the familiar movements of the game coming back to him like second nature. He pushed himself harder than ever, determined to prove to himself and his team that he was worthy of his place on varsity. The practice continued for hours, but Damian barely noticed the time passing.

The air was heavy with the same moist stillness as if a storm was coming. The sun was barely more than a glow above the horizon, but it was already hot, and the air was still. The players gathered around Coach Dean, kneeled, and waited for their coach's dismissal. They had finished practice; now, they slumped in relief.

Jared tapped Damian's shoulder and, in a low tone, said, "Jesus, it's hot! Do you think your mom could give me a ride home? I need a cold shower or something."

Trying not to laugh, Damian quietly said, "Yeah, of course. No problem. I need to do that same, man." The two snickered.

"Great job today, boys! I saw a lot of good things today, but it's only the beginning! We need this effort every day. One practice isn't enough. Consistency! We need consistency. That's how you get better! A runner doesn't run one mile, one time and think they can take on the Boston Marathon. The grind, day after day, until that marathon, is just another day at the ballpark. Now, go home, rest up, and drink lots of water. It is the best time of the year, boys. Enjoy this August heat."

As they limped off the field, Damian's gaze landed on a girl sitting alone in the bleachers. She sat with one leg crossed over the other, her long, unruly curls tumbling down her shoulders like a wild river. Her lips curled into a sly grin that sent shivers down Damian's spine. Following Damian's fascination, Jared nudged him and whispered, "Go talk to her, dude." With sweaty palms, Damian approached her, unsure of what to say.

"Hey there," he said, trying to sound casual.

The girl grinned up at him. "Hey," she said, her voice husky and low. "You're Damian, right?"

Damian was surprised she knew his name, but he nodded anyway. "Yeah, that's me. Who are you?"

The girl's smile widened. "I'm Carmen," she said, and Damian couldn't help but feel a jolt of attraction run through him. "Just moved here over the Summer, and I'm trying out for the cheer team. You're famous, you know?"

"Am I?" Damian said, now grinning as well.

"Yup, the girls were talking about who was the best player on the team, and your name came up. Something about following your brother but in another sport or something?

"Wow, flattering I guess," Damian replied, now less excited.

They exchanged pleasantries, their voices carrying through the air like birds in conversation. As the minutes wore on and the sun began to sink lower in the sky, Jared gave a subtle nod to signal that it was his cue to leave. They promised to meet again soon, quickly exchanging numbers before going their separate ways. As Carmen walked away, her confident stride caught his eye once again. She was unlike any other girl he had met - secure in her identity and unafraid to share her opinions. She clearly had a strong sense of direction in life, and he couldn't help but admire her for it.

"Jeez, you're totally under her spell now!" Jared teased as they headed toward Damian's mother's car. Damian gave his buddy a playful shove, feeling slightly self-conscious that he may be right.

The car windows were rolled down, but the hot summer air still felt suffocating as they rode to Jared's house to drop him off. His mind was consumed by thoughts of Carmen—her dark blue eyes, her soft voice. He couldn't help but wonder about her past and whether she shared his feelings. Suddenly, Jared's voice broke through his thoughts, returning him to reality.

"Dang Casanova, look at you. She's got you wrapped around her finger already, man. You've got it wrong, don't you?"

Damian chuckled, feeling a little embarrassed. "No, I don't know, man. There's something about her."

Jared grinned. "Well, don't screw it up then. Get her number and answer that door."

Damian nodded, feeling a sense of determination. He was going to see Carmen again, and he was going to make a move.

Damian's face lit up with excitement as he asked Jared, "Are you excited for the season you will have? I think they will start throwing the ball your way this year."

J chuckled, scrunching his nose as he nodded vigorously. "Oh, I'm stoked! I can't wait to earn a starting spot. You already got yours, so I can't let you have all the fun."

Damian grinned and changed the subject. "Excited for school?"

Jared tilted his head to the side and rolled his eyes with a half laugh before nodding. "No, not at all, Bro. But…you know. You have to do what you have to do. Hopefully, we have a lot of classes together again; I'll probably need your help."

Damian smiled warmly, "When do you not need my help?" The two laughed together.

When they arrived at Jared's house, his mother met them on the front porch. The smell of alcohol and something akin to melted plastic hit Damian's nose like a punch. On the front porch stood Jared's mother, her stern expression softened by a hint of concern as she watched Damian's discomfort. They said their goodbyes, and Jared turned to leave and go into the house. Damian couldn't help but notice the worn wooden steps and peeling paint on the porch railings. As soon as the door closed behind them, Damian took a deep breath, grateful to be away from the overwhelming smell in the air outside.

Damian watched as Jared ran into his house, only to be ignored by his mother. He knocked on the door to ensure she saw him and waved, but his mother turned away and walked into the kitchen. The screen door banged shut behind her. Damian felt terrible and didn't understand how she could act so differently at work than at home.

As they drove down the road, Damian's mother looked over at him and said, "You're a good friend to Jared," Damian was taken aback, unsure what she meant. She continued, "He's got so much going on in his life, but he needs strong people like you and Michael to keep him focused. Be patient with him." Damian thought about her words as they cruised along the highway. Some of him wanted to be that kind of friend for Jared, but he was curious if he could ever live up to those expectations.

As they pulled into their driveway, Damian thought about Carmen. He wondered if it was too soon to message her or if he should play it cool and try the next day. Taking a deep breath, he decided to go for it.

Damian showered, then, while in his room, quickly took out his phone and typed out a message: "Hey there. It was great meeting you today. Hopefully, we can hang out soon – Damian." His fingers felt heavy as he hit send, almost as if he feared the message wouldn't get through. But soon enough, his phone lit up with an incoming message from Carmen: "Hey there! Good to meet you, too! Yeah, we definitely should soon. What's your practice schedule looking like?"

Damian smiled at the sight of her name and quickly typed back a response, excited that she seemed to express the same interest as him.

The first day of the new school year had finally arrived, and Damian felt a sense of comfort. Last year, he was anxious about attending high school and making his name known. Now, he felt more secure, not that there wouldn't be difficulties, but he was sure he could face them without fear.

With Lee off to college this year, Jared took his place in the car with Damian and his father as they made their way to school. As it was last year, the line to drop off students was very long. Despite being in good company, Jared couldn't muster the same enthusiasm for the day as Damian.

"Another year, boys. Only so many of these first days are left." Damian's father said. Damian whipped the sleepiness from his eyes.

"Yeah, we're sophomores now. Can you believe that?" Damian asked Jared.

"Yeah, sure. It's cool. We still have the same math together, right?"

"Right, just like last year, but it looks like Mr. Anderson is our actual teacher this year, not just a fill-in."

"He's a cool dude. Glad for that." Jared said as he leaned his head against the window.

"Nothing worth doing is ever easy." Damian's father spoke firmly, and his mouth turned up in a half-smile. "I hated going to school when I was your age, but it all goes so fast, and then you're out into the world. Keep pushing through, and don't give up—it's worth it in the end."

Damian smiled, feeling the truth of these words sink in. His father had been right about freshmen year: one moment, he'd arrived, and the next, he was packing for summer break. And this year would be as fleeting, soon gone before Damian knew it.

The car slowly pulled to a stop, and Damian immediately grabbed his bag from the backseat before saying goodbye to his father. As he and Jared exited the vehicle, Theresa awaited them outside the school's entrance. She warmly embraced both boys before they all turned toward the school together.

Damian stood with his two friends, watching students stream through the doors. He grinned at Jared and Theresa, saying, "Guys, let's enjoy this year together. No fighting or stupid pranks this year. Let's enjoy ourselves and look out for each other." Jared raised an eyebrow at Damian before turning to Theresa, who beamed and nodded in agreement. The three friends entered their second year of high school together, ready for whatever challenges the new school year would bring.

CHAPTER 23 – MR. FROST

The morning sunlight filtered through the gaps in the office blinds, casting long shadows across Damian's desk. He sat, fingers poised over his keyboard, staring at the glowing monitor. The low hum of the air conditioning and the distant chatter of his coworkers created a white noise that seemed to blur the edges of his concentration.

Damian's eyes flicked to the clock on his computer screen. 9:15 AM. He'd been at work for over an hour but felt like he'd accomplished nothing. The stack of papers beside him seemed to mock his efforts, a constant reminder of the monotonous tasks that filled his days.

With a sigh, he pushed back from his desk and stood up, stretching his arms above his head. His gaze drifted to the window, where he could see the bustling city below. People hurried along the sidewalks, their purposeful strides sharply contrasting with the listlessness he felt.

"Good morning Mr. Frost."

Damian turned to see Gabi, one of his coworkers, peering over the top of his cubicle. Her curly hair was pulled back in a messy bun, and she wore a sympathetic smile.

"Hey, Gabi," Damian responded, forcing a smile of his own.

"I heard about your friend," she said softly. "I'm so sorry for your loss."

Damian nodded, the familiar ache of grief tightening in his chest. "Thank you," he managed.

"If you need anything, let me know, okay?" Gabi offered before disappearing back to her workspace.

Damian sank back into his chair, Jared's absence pressing down on him. It had been weeks since the funeral, but the reality of his friend's death still felt surreal. He reached for his phone, half-expecting to see a message from Jared, before remembering that those messages would never come again.

The morning seemed to drag on, each task blending into the next. Damian found himself going through the motions, his mind elsewhere. He thought about his students from last year, wondering how they were doing with their new teacher. He thought about Mr. Anderson and the other teachers at Crossroads High, imagining the buzz of excitement that always came with the school year.

As lunchtime approached, Damian decided he needed a change of scenery. He grabbed his jacket and headed for the elevator, intent on finding a quiet spot in a nearby park to clear his head.

The elevator dinged, and the doors slid open. Damian stepped inside, only to find himself face-to-face with a familiar figure.

"Carmen?" he exclaimed, surprise coloring his voice.

The woman looked up from her phone, her eyes widening in recognition. "Damian? Oh my god, is that you?"

They stared at each other for a moment before breaking into laughter. Carmen stepped forward, pulling Damian into a warm hug.

"I can't believe it's you," she said as they parted. "What are you doing here?"

"I work here," Damian replied, still processing the unexpected encounter. "In the contracting office. What about you?"

"I'm in HR," Carmen explained. "Seventh floor. How long have you been here?"

"A few months," Damian said. "I had no idea you worked here too."

The elevator reached the ground floor, and they stepped out together. As they walked through the lobby, Damian found himself studying Carmen. She looked different from how he remembered her in high school - more confident, more self-assured. Her hair was now shorter, cut into a stylish bob framed by her face.

"Hey," Carmen said, interrupting his thoughts. "I was heading out for lunch. Want to join me? We have a lot of catching up to do."

Damian hesitated for a moment before nodding. "Yeah, that sounds great."

They found a small café a block away from the office building. As they settled into a corner table with their sandwiches, Damian felt a sense of déjà vu. It was like being back in high school, sharing lunch with a friend.

"So," Carmen began, sipping her iced tea. "Last I heard, you were teaching. What brought you to the exciting world of government contracting?"

Damian chuckled, the sound tinged with a hint of bitterness. "It's a long story," he said. "Short version? Teaching didn't work out the way I hoped it would."

Carmen nodded thoughtfully. "I understand. Sometimes our dreams don't align with reality."

"What about you?" Damian asked, eager to shift the focus away from himself. "How did you end up in HR?"

Carmen laughed. "Honestly? I fell into it. After college, I was looking for any job I could get. I started as a temp in the HR department, and it just… fit. You know what I mean?"

As they talked, Damian relaxed for the first time in weeks. There was something comforting about reconnecting with someone from his past, someone who knew him before he was Mr. Frost before he was a failed teacher before he lost Jared.

"I heard about your friend," Carmen said softly, reaching across the table to touch Damian's hand. "I'm so sorry, Damian."

Damian swallowed hard, fighting back the lump in his throat. "Thanks," he managed. "It's been… hard."

Carmen squeezed his hand gently. "I can't even imagine. How are you holding up?"

Damian took a deep breath, considering his answer. "Some days are better than others," he admitted. "It's just… I keep thinking about all the things I should have done differently. All the times I could have reached out could have been there for him more."

"Damian," Carmen said, her voice firm but kind. "You can't blame yourself. We all have our paths to walk. You were a good friend to Jared. I remember that much from high school."

Damian nodded, grateful for her words, even if he didn't fully believe them. "Thanks, Carmen. It means a lot to hear that."

As they finished their lunch, Damian was reluctant to return to the office. Being with Carmen, talking about the past and the present, had awakened something in him - a sense of possibility that had been dormant for too long.

"We should do this again sometime," Carmen said as they returned to the office building. "It's been nice catching up."

"Yeah, it has," Damian agreed. "Maybe next time we can grab dinner after work?"

Carmen smiled a warm, genuine expression that made Damian's heart skip a beat. "I'd like that," she said.

As they parted ways in the lobby, a whirlwind of emotions swept through Damian. The grief over Jared was still there, a constant ache in his chest. But alongside it was a flicker of something else—hope, maybe—or at least the possibility of hope.

The afternoon passed in a blur of emails and spreadsheets. Damian found his mind wandering, replaying his conversation with Carmen. He thought about the path that had led him here, to this job that felt more like a holding pattern than a career. He thought about his students, about the passion he'd felt in front of a classroom.

As the workday ended, Damian decided. He quickly emailed his supervisor, Lauren, asking for a meeting the next day. Then, gathering his things, he headed out of the office.

Instead of going straight home, Damian drove to the cemetery where Jared was buried. The sun was setting as he walked through the quiet grounds, casting long shadows across the rows of headstones.

He found Jared's grave quickly, the polished granite still shiny and new. Damian stood there for a long moment, hands shoved deep in his pockets, unsure what to say.

"Hey, man," he finally said, his voice barely above a whisper. "I miss you. I'm sorry I haven't been by more often. Things have been… complicated."

Damian sank onto the grass, leaning back against a nearby

tree. "I saw Carmen today," he continued, finding comfort in talking to Jared, even if his friend couldn't respond. "Remember her from high school? She works in the same building as me now. It was… nice. Reminded me of old times."

He fell silent for a moment, watching as the last rays of sunlight painted the sky in shades of orange and pink. "I've been thinking a lot about teaching lately," Damian admitted. "About the kids, about making a difference. I don't know, Jared. I feel like I gave up too easily. Like I let fear and doubt win."

The words came easier now, flowing out of him like a river breaking through a dam. "I keep hearing Mr. Anderson's voice in my head, you know? 'When fortune knocks, answer the door.' I think… I think maybe I've been ignoring some knocks lately."

As the light faded and the first stars began to appear in the sky, Damian felt a sense of peace settle over him. It wasn't the absence of grief or doubt but rather a coexistence - an acknowledgment that life could contain both sorrow and hope, both loss and new beginnings.

"I'm going to try again, Jared," Damian said, rising to his feet. "I don't know if it'll work out, but I have to try. I owe it to myself. And… I think I owe it to you, too. To live the life we always talked about, to make a difference."

He pressed his hand against the cold stone of Jared's headstone. "I'll make you proud, buddy. I promise."

The next morning, Damian arrived at the office early, his stomach knotted with nerves and anticipation. He'd spent half the night updating his resume and browsing job listings for teaching positions. It felt both terrifying and exhilarating to consider returning to education.

At precisely 9:30 AM, Damian knocked on Lauren's office

door.

"Come in," she called.

Damian took a deep breath and stepped inside. Lauren looked up from her computer, a warm smile on her face.

"Damian," she said. "What can I do for you?"

Damian sat across from her desk with his hands clasped tightly in his lap. "Lauren," he began, "I wanted to talk to you about my future here."

Lauren's expression turned serious. "Is everything okay, Damian? You've been doing great work."

"Thank you," Damian said. "I appreciate that. And I'm grateful for the opportunity you've given me here. But…" He paused, gathering his courage. "The truth is, I don't think this is where I'm meant to be long-term."

Understanding dawned in Lauren's eyes. "You're thinking about returning to teaching, aren't you?"

Damian nodded, relieved that she'd made the connection. "Yes. I've been thinking a lot lately, and I realized that teaching is where my passion lies. It's where I feel I can make the biggest difference."

Lauren leaned back in her chair, considering his words. "I can't say I'm not disappointed to hear that," she said. "You're a valuable member of our team. But I respect your decision to pursue your passion."

"Thank you for understanding," Damian said. "I was hoping… well, I was wondering if it would be okay to start applying for teaching positions while continuing to work here. I don't want to leave you in the dush, and I know it might take some time to find the right opportunity."

Lauren nodded. "I think that's a reasonable approach. We can keep this conversation between us for now. And Damian?

If you need a reference for your applications, I'd happily provide one."

Damian felt a wave of relief wash over him. "Thank you, Lauren. That means a lot to me."

As he left Lauren's office, Damian felt lighter than he had in months. He returned to his desk with a new sense of purpose driving him. He opened his email, intending to start drafting cover letters, when he noticed a new message in his inbox.

The sender's name made his heart skip a beat: Mr. Anderson.

With shaking hands, Damian opened the email:

"Dear Damian,

I hope this email finds you well. I've been thinking about you lately and wanted to check-in. How are you finding your new career? I must admit, the halls of Crossroads High aren't quite the same without your enthusiasm and dedication.

I also wanted to let you know that we're anticipating some openings in our English department in August, though it'll be posted earlier. If you're interested in returning to teaching, I'd be happy to put in a good word for you.

Best regards,

Mr. Anderson"

Damian read the email three times, hardly daring to believe it. He glanced up, his gaze landing on a small, framed quote on his desk - a gift from his father when he started this job. It read: "When fortune knocks, answer the door."

With a smile, Damian began to type his response to Mr. Anderson. As his fingers flew across the keyboard, he felt a sense of rightness, of coming full circle. He thought of Jared, Carmen, and all the twists and turns that had led him to this moment.

Damian realized that life was a series of doors—some that closed, others that opened unexpectedly. The trick was having the courage to walk through them and seize the opportunities that presented themselves.

As he hit 'send' on his email to Mr. Anderson, Damian felt excited for what lay ahead. He didn't know exactly where this new path would lead, but he was ready to find out—ready to answer the knock of fortune, wherever it might take him.

The office buzzed around him, phones ringing and printers whirring, but Damian barely noticed. In his mind, he was already standing in front of a classroom, ready to inspire a new generation of students. Ready to make a difference, one lesson at a time.

And somewhere, he liked to think, Jared was watching and smiling, proud of his friend for finding his way back where he belonged.